Clint estimated the sniper was only about three hundred yards away, beyond the accurate range of the Gunsmith's Springfield.

Clint decided to give the sniper a surprise. He aimed the Springfield like a motor, pointing it at the peak of the mountain. Clint aimed high and hoped the bullet would descend in an arch to strike near the sniper's position. The principle worked with field artillery, but the Gunsmith didn't know if it would apply to a rifle round. He'd find out.

The Gunsmith squeezed the trigger . . .

Don't miss any of the lusty, hard-riding action in the Charter Western series, THE GUNSMITH:

THE GUNSMITH #1: MACKLIN'S WOMEN
THE GUNSMITH #2: THE CHINESE GUNMEN
THE GUNSMITH #3: THE WOMAN HUNT
THE GUNSMITH #4: THE GUNS OF ABILENE
THE GUNSMITH #5: THREE GUNS FOR GLORY
THE GUNSMITH #6: LEADTOWN
THE GUNSMITH #7: THE LONGHORN WAR
THE GUNSMITH #8: QUANAH'S REVENGE
THE GUNSMITH #9: HEAVYWEIGHT GUN
THE GUNSMITH #10: NEW ORLEANS FIRE
THE GUNSMITH #11: ONE-HANDED GUN
THE GUNSMITH #12: THE CANADIAN PAYROLL
THE GUNSMITH #13: DRAW TO AN INSIDE DEATH
THE GUNSMITH #14: DEAD MAN'S HAND
THE GUNSMITH #15: BANDIT GOLD
THE GUNSMITH #16: BUCKSKINS AND SIX-GUNS
THE GUNSMITH #17: SILVER WAR
THE GUNSMITH #18: HIGH NOON AT LANCASTER
THE GUNSMITH #19: BANDIDO BLOOD
THE GUNSMITH #20: THE DODGE CITY GANG
THE GUNSMITH #21: SASQUATCH HUNT
THE GUNSMITH #22: BULLETS AND BALLOTS
THE GUNSMITH #23: THE RIVERBOAT GANG
THE GUNSMITH #24: KILLER GRIZZLY
THE GUNSMITH #25: NORTH OF THE BORDER
THE GUNSMITH #26: EAGLE'S GAP
THE GUNSMITH #27: CHINATOWN HELL
THE GUNSMITH #28: THE PANHANDLE SEARCH
THE GUNSMITH #29: WILDCAT ROUNDUP
THE GUNSMITH #30: THE PONDEROSA WAR
THE GUNSMITH #31: TROUBLE RIDES A FAST HORSE

And coming next month:

THE GUNSMITH #33: THE POSSE

THE GUNSMITH 32
DYNAMITE JUSTICE

J.R. ROBERTS

CHARTER BOOKS, NEW YORK

THE GUNSMITH #32: DYNAMITE JUSTICE

A Charter Book/published by arrangement with the author

PRINTING HISTORY
Charter Original/September 1984

All rights reserved.
Copyright © 1984 by Robert J. Randisi
This book may not be reproduced in whole
or in part, by mimeograph or any other means,
without permission. For information address:
The Berkley Publishing Group,
200 Madison Avenue, New York, N.Y. 10016

ISBN: 0-441-30911-9

Charter Books are published by The Berkley Publishing Group,
200 Madison Avenue, New York, N.Y. 10016.

PRINTED IN THE UNITED STATES OF AMERICA

*Dedicated to
David Cheney*

ONE

The town of Holden was growing. The wooden skeletons of several buildings still under construction were proof of that. Clint Adams smiled when he saw the number of people in the streets—lots of people meant lots of business for a traveling gunsmith.

Following a personal custom of courtesy, Clint paid a visit to the local sheriff. A former lawman himself, Clint realized a sheriff likes to know about strangers in town. Especially one with the Gunsmith's reputation.

Clint Adams had not chosen to be known as the Gunsmith. The monicker had been given to him years ago by a newspaperman who wanted a colorful angle to a story about Deputy Adams. The journalist discovered Clint's hobby was repairing and modifying firearms. That's when he was first labeled *the Gunsmith*.

Of course, Clint's fame as the Gunsmith revolved around his speed and accuracy with a gun, not his ability as a craftsman. After eighteen years as a lawman, Clint quit wearing a badge. Ironically, he then became a genuine gunsmith and traveled throughout the West in a wagon which served as a gunsmith shop.

Clint spent most of his time on the trail, traveling from town to town, his constant companion and closest friend a big black Arabian gelding named Duke. The horse was his most prized possession, one he valued second only to his own life.

Clint enjoyed as much freedom as any man who must work for a living—more so because he had saved a considerable nest egg over the years and could retire if he continued to build the size of his savings. Yet Clint was in no hurry to settle down. He drifted because it was his choice.

Unlike most drifters, Clint wasn't looking for anything special—he'd already found it. The Gunsmith was free and mobile. He could do as he pleased with no family ties or personal commitments to restrain him. There was no point in planning to get married one day and raise a family. No man with a reputation like his could ever hope to live out his remaining years in peace.

Sheriff Luke Calhune, the chief lawman in Holden, had heard a lot about the Gunsmith. Calhune was stunned when the tall, slender stranger entered his office and introduced himself as Clint Adams. The Gunsmith didn't appear to be a typical gunhawk. Clad in denim and trail dust, Clint didn't seem much different than most saddlebums drifting through town. Only the jagged scar on his left cheek and the way he wore his gun suggested Clint was accustomed to violence.

Unlike some lawmen who resented the Gunsmith, Calhune appreciated Clint's visit. He knew that the Gunsmith had a knack for getting into trouble. Clint never started it, but he usually ended it—bringing his problems to a swift and final conclusion. Calhune understood that the Gunsmith had never killed a man in cold blood or accepted money as a hired gunman.

The sheriff's attitude proved to be the start of Clint's

DYNAMITE JUSTICE

two days of good luck in Holden. The local gunsmith had died almost a year ago so Clint had plenty of customers who needed to have firearms repaired or modified. The Gunsmith got more business in two days in Holden than he usually received in a month.

Of course, what good is new-found wealth if a man can't enjoy it? The Gunsmith spent most of the second evening in the local saloon where he found a friendly game of draw poker in progress. To Clint's relief, all the players were honest. And the Gunsmith's luck continued to hold.

Clint won several hands, more than doubling his money. The two card players who lost the most decided to quit while they still had a pair of boots to call their own. The others were willing to gamble on getting their money back, but they had more stubborn determination than good sense. Both tended to bet recklessly and neither paid much attention to the odds.

The Gunsmith would probably have cleaned them out if the game had continued. He was shuffling the deck for the next deal when Sheriff Calhune approached the table.

"Howdy, Mr. Adams," the lawman began. "Figured I might find you here."

"Been looking for me, Sheriff?" Clint inquired. He noticed Calhune carried a sawed-off shotgun.

"That I have," Calhune nodded. He glanced at the stack of coins and paper bills in front of the Gunsmith. "Appears you ain't done badly tonight."

"You didn't come in here to see how I was doing at cards," Clint remarked. "What can I do for you, Sheriff?"

"Like to have a word with you in private."

"You fellas mind if I call it a night?" the Gunsmith asked the other card players.

"Maybe somebody else will have a chance now," one of them muttered sourly.

"Thanks for the game," Clint said as he raked up his winnings.

The Gunsmith followed Calhune outside. The streets of Holden were quiet. The only light came from the moon and stars and from the windows of the saloon. The streets were deserted. The two men were the only people on the plankwalks that night.

"I got a problem, Mr. Adams," Calhune admitted.

"Didn't figure you were carrying that scattergun just for exercise," Clint commented.

"Wondered if maybe you could help me out, Mr. Adams."

"Can't say until you tell me what you need," the Gunsmith replied. "And call me Clint. Mr. Adams was my father. Okay?"

"Well, I'm afeared there might be some trouble from the Waldren family," the sheriff confessed. "They're more like a clan than a family. Got some mighty strange customs, but they tend to keep to themselves most of the time."

"I take it these Waldrens have done something to change your mind about them," Clint guessed.

"You might say that," the lawman nodded. "Turns out the Waldrens sort of had their own personal slave girl tucked away up on their mountain."

"What?" the Gunsmith frowned. "A slave girl? Didn't anybody ever get around to telling the Waldrens that Abe Lincoln abolished slavery some time ago?"

"Well, this ain't exactly slavery like they had on the plantations afore the War Between the States,"

Calhune answered. "But I don't know what else to call it. Maybe you could talk to the gal."

"A real honest to God slave girl?" the Gunsmith rolled his eyes. "I can hardly wait."

TWO

Sheriff Calhune took Clint Adams to his office. The lawman knocked on the door and announced who he was. A bolt was pulled back and the door opened.

"Thank God you're back," a feminine voice said, her tone revealing considerable relief.

"Don't fret, Ellie," Calhune urged as he led Clint into the unlit room.

"Who is this with you?" she asked with nervous concern.

"He's a friend," the sheriff assured her.

The lawman struck a match to light the kerosene lamp on his desk. Pale yellow light flooded the office. Clint raised his eyebrows with surprise when he saw the girl. She was small and thin with a shapeless sack dress hung over her slender frame.

Ellie's skin was the color of a copper penny. Long silky black hair framed her lean cheeks. Soft brown eyes stared up at Clint above the girl's high cheekbones.

"Ellie Dove," Calhune began. "This is Clint Adams. Ever hear of him?"

"No, sir," she replied sheepishly.

"Well, Clint is better known as the Gunsmith," the

sheriff began. "He's probably the fastest gunman in the West. Maybe in the whole world . . ."

"Oh, hell," Clint groaned. "Don't encourage those tales about me."

"I was about to add that you've got a reputation as a man of honor," Calhune stated. "And you don't mind helping folks out from time to time."

"I wish you'd explain what this is all about, Sheriff," the Gunsmith sighed.

"Okay," the lawman began. "Ellie here is a Ute Indian, but she's also a Christian educated by a missionary church."

"Before my parents died," the girl explained, "they were converted to the true faith and left the tribe because the rest of the Utes continued to practice a false and evil religion."

"I wouldn't say what the Utes believe is necessarily false or evil," Clint said. "But I'm not much for arguing with folks about religion. Now, will somebody just tell me what the hell is going on?"

"A couple weeks ago," Calhune explained, "Ellie was out gathering firewood for the mission when the Waldrens seen her. They just kidnapped the girl like she was a stray dog and took her to their home up on the hill. Then they forced her to . . . well, sort of join the family."

"You mean one of them took her as an unwilling mate?" Clint asked bluntly.

"Not exactly," Calhune said awkwardly. "You see, the Waldrens lost all their womenfolk. Old Jed's wife died a couple years ago and his daughter died about three months back. That left just the old man and his three sons."

"And they missed having a woman's touch around their place so much they went out and captured a girl?"

The Gunsmith shook his head. "Sounds pretty far-fetched to me, Sheriff."

"The Waldrens worked their women like slaves," the lawman explained. "And they—they must've practiced incest."

"You mean sister and brother?" Clint frowned. "Father and daughter? Mother and son?"

"Incest ain't all that rare among some of these hill clans," Calhune stated. "Folks just don't like to talk about it much. From what Ellie tells me, the Waldrens is capable of worse things than screwin' with kinfolk."

"Such as?" Clint asked.

"Jed and his sons told me if I disobeyed them I'd get the same treatment they gave their own women," Ellie replied.

"What's that?"

"The mother got real sick and wasn't able to work," Ellie explained. "The men had lost interest in keeping her around, since she couldn't do for them anymore. They simply let her die. Then the boys bragged to me that they got drunk one night, and the two older ones went for their sister. When she didn't do what they wanted, they slapped her. They beat her worse than they intended."

"Jesus," Clint muttered. He turned to Calhune. "Why don't you get a posse together and go arrest those bastards?"

"The only proof I've got is Ellie's testimony, Clint," the sheriff answered. "And she's an Indian. You know what that means, don't you?"

The Gunsmith nodded. "Most folks won't take her word against a family of whites. I know that's how it usually works, but everybody in town must know what kind of trash the Waldrens are."

"They don't know a damn thing about the Waldrens," Calhune told him. "Hell, the clan just stays up there on Waldren Mountain most of the time. Nobody around here associates with them except to buy some corn liquor from old Jed. The two older boys sometimes hire out as farmhands, but they've never given anybody reason to complain about them. Always seemed to be hard workin' and honest, according to the fellers what hired them."

"The youngest son is the worst," Ellie said bitterly. "The others are illiterate, but Jed Boy can read and write. He's even familiar with parts of the Bible, but he ignores what the Good Book says. The old man is very proud of that one. He thinks Jed Boy will be governor of the state someday."

"That's more than anybody in Holden would figure the kid is capable of," Calhune remarked. "But the local school marm thinks Jed Boy might write dime novels or something like that if he tries hard enough."

"Charming family," Clint said dryly. "So what are you going to do, Sheriff?"

"I figure those crazy sons of bitches might just come here to reclaim what they figure belongs to them."

"Meaning Ellie." The Gunsmith nodded. "What do you want me to do?"

"Well"—Calhune sighed—"my deputy is out of town. Went to Denver to marry a gal he's been writing to for more than a year. I can purely use some help, Clint."

"You want to deputize me?" Clint frowned.

"Heard you haven't worn a badge for years."

"You heard right," the Gunsmith confirmed.

"Well, all we need is a place for Ellie to stay where the Waldrens won't look for her," Calhune began. "Could you just take Ellie to the hotel and hide her in your room?"

"That's sort of like putting a bandage on a bullet hole without taking the slug out first," the Gunsmith stated. "It'll help for a while, but it won't solve the problem."

"Just take care of her until my deputy gets back," Calhune urged.

"How long is that going to be?" Clint demanded. "I'm planning to leave town tomorrow morning. Figure I'll head up to Dublin and see if I can strike up some business there."

"Dublin?" Calhune frowned. "That's the place where all those Irish immigrants settled."

"You hear something bad about the place?" Clint asked.

"Not really." The sheriff shrugged. "Just those Irish folks come from back East. Most of 'em are from Pennsylvania. Reckon you've heard about all the trouble they caused back there."

"You mean the Molly Maguires?" Clint inquired. "I heard that outfit is just about extinct. Most of them have been rounded up and either hanged or thrown in prison. Besides, only a small minority of the Irish coal miners in Pennsylvania are involved with those owlhoots anyway."

"Reckon you're right." Calhune sighed. "And Dublin ain't my problem."

"And *my* problem does not concern Mr. Adams," Ellie commented simply.

"I didn't say I wouldn't help," Clint told her. "But I can't take care of you forever."

"Just for tonight?" Calhune asked. "We'll figure something else to do in the morning."

"Okay," the Gunsmith sighed. "I'll do it."

THREE

Sheriff Calhune entered the hotel lobby. He approached the desk clerk, Joel Cabot, and told him a rope was dangling from a second story window at the rear of the building. Cabot was outraged by the possibility that a tenant might be trying to sneak out without paying his bill. The clerk grabbed a revolver from under his desk and dashed to the side door. The lawman followed, urging Cabot to calm down.

The Gunsmith and Ellie Dove stood on the plankwalk across the street. Clint grinned when he heard Calhune tell Cabot to restrict his vigilante notions and to watch his language in case there were any ladies listening at their windows.

"If the sheriff ever decides to quit wearing a badge," Clint whispered to Ellie, "he could probably make a living as a snake oil salesman. Let's go."

The pair entered the empty lobby and quickly mounted the stairs to the second floor. Clint led the girl to his room. Inside, he pulled the window shade down and locked the door before he struck a match to light the coal-oil lamp.

"Better stay away from the window and don't talk too loud," the Gunsmith told Ellie.

"You seem quite concerned, Mr. Adams," she said with surprise.

"Just call me Clint," the Gunsmith answered. "And you bet I'm taking the Waldrens seriously. We could have just bribed the desk clerk to let you come upstairs with me. Calhune must figure the Waldrens are pretty nasty to insist on going to this much trouble to sneak you up here instead. The sheriff clearly thinks they might wring information out of the clerk if the fella knows you're here."

"They would not hesitate to do exactly that," the girl confirmed. "And they'd certainly kill him if they thought he lied to them. The Waldrens are brutes. You have no idea how cruel they can be."

"Must have been pretty hard for you," Clint remarked.

"I only pray that that nightmare is over," Ellie replied as she sat on the edge of the bed.

"Where will you go when you leave Holden?" the Gunsmith asked, removing a bedroll from his gear stored in one corner of the room.

"I do not know," the girl answered. "But I can not return to the mission now."

"Why not?" Clint inquired as he laid his blankets on the floor.

"Because I am unclean," Ellie said sadly. "The Waldrens . . . they violated me."

"But that wasn't your fault," Clint told her. "Nobody can blame you because you were raped by those bastards."

"I should have taken my own life rather than surrender my virtue to such beasts," Ellie said, shaking her head with despair.

"Don't be silly," the Gunsmith urged as he folded a

sheepskin jacket and placed it on the bedroll. "You're a Christian, right? Didn't they ever tell you that suicide is a sin?"

"So is fornication." The girl sighed.

"At least it's not so permanent. Hell, Ellie. You can't be serious about blaming yourself for what happened?"

"I suppose my main concern is that no decent man will ever want me now," Ellie remarked.

"That's absurd," Clint told her. "Any decent man wouldn't condemn you because you were a victim of rapists."

"But I am no longer a virgin," the girl stated, tears trickling down her cheeks.

"So what?" The Gunsmith smiled. "The only men who insist that a girl be a virgin are fellas that doubt their own prowess in bed. They're afraid they'll be unfavorably compared to a lady's previous lovers."

"Are you so insecure, Clint?" the girl asked.

"Me?" He chuckled. "Well, I'm fairly satisfied with who I am. I don't waste much time comparing myself with anybody else at anything."

"Including making love?"

"Reckon I don't worry about my . . . uh, ability when it comes to that subject," Clint admitted.

"Then why have you put those blankets on the floor?" she demanded.

"I'm going to sleep there," Clint replied, confused by her question.

"Why?"

"Well, I figured you'd want to sleep in the bed," he said.

"Wouldn't you rather sleep in the bed than on the floor?"

"After all you've been through I didn't think you'd want to share a bed with a man."

"Well, I no longer have my virginity to guard. And from what you've just said, I don't think that I fear finding a decent man. I would be comforted to share a bed with a strong, kind man such as you. You have not harmed me, Clint," Ellie declared. "Why would I object to your company?"

"I . . ." The Gunsmith sighed hopelessly. "I swear a fella can never understand how a woman will react to anything."

"You're rejecting me, Clint?" the girl demanded.

"Oh, for crissake," Clint muttered, uncertain of what to say or do. He wondered if Ellie's ordeal with the Waldrens may have rattled her brain a little loose.

"Do you object to me because I'm a soiled woman or because I'm a Ute Indian?" Ellie asked.

"I don't object to you at all, Ellie," Clint assured her.

"Have you ever slept with an Indian girl?" she asked as she suddenly rose from the bed.

"Yes, I have," the Gunsmith admitted. "More than once, as a matter of fact."

"Wasn't it as satisfying with an Indian as it is with a white woman?"

"How satisfying a woman is in bed doesn't have anything to do with that," Clint replied.

"Then you don't like white women better?" the girl asked as she reached both hands to her shoulders.

"Well, I like fried chicken." Clint smiled. "But I also like roast beef and buffalo steaks. Women are sort of the same."

"Which do you like best?" Ellie asked, slipping the straps of the dress from her shoulders.

The garment fell to her ankles. Clint stared at her. When a woman strips in front of a man, it would be silly—to say nothing of insulting—not to take a good look. Everything the Gunsmith saw looked just fine, too.

The shapeless burlap dress had concealed a lovely body. Ellie's breasts jutted free, the brown nipples pointing at Clint Adams. Some ribs were visible beneath the firm mounds of tempting flesh. Her long thin waist seemed to extend directly to her legs with barely a trace of hips between.

"Well?" she asked. "Which do you like better?"

"That sort of depends on what whets my appetite." The Gunsmith smiled.

Clint approached Ellie and took her in his arms. He kissed her left shoulder. The girl hugged his waist as Clint slowly moved his lips to her neck.

He ran the tip of his tongue along the curve of Ellie's jaw. She gasped with pleasure. Clint nibbled on her earlobe gently while Ellie fumbled with the buttons of his trousers. She unfastened the pants fly and freed his erect penis.

The Gunsmith broke the embrace and unbuckled his gunbelt. He hung it over the headboard and quickly stripped off his clothing. Ellie sprawled naked across the mattress and watched him disrobe. She clearly liked what she saw.

Clint Adams was not a boy, although he appeared to be at least ten years younger than his true forty-plus age. He was leanly muscled and his slender physique remained strong and fit.

Numerous scars marred his flesh. The Gunsmith had lost count of how many times he had narrowly escaped death. The scars were physical evidence of just a few of such encounters, each scar a constant reminder etched into Clint's skin. *You are mortal*, these tattoos warned.

The Gunsmith joined Ellie in the bed. His hands slid across her breasts. He thumbed the nipples gently, feeling them stiffen under his touch. Slowly, his fingers traveled along Ellie's smooth, flat belly while his lips moved to her breasts.

The girl moaned with pleasure as the Gunsmith teased her nipples with his teeth and tongue. His fingers slipped between her thighs and stroked soft warm flesh. Ellie reached for Clint's hard member and guided it into her. The Gunsmith skillfully continued to kiss her neck and breasts while he increased the tempo of his thrusts.

He paced himself as he slowly brought the girl to her limit. Ellie cried out in joy when an orgasm caused a wild convulsion to ripple through her body. The Gunsmith rode the girl to a second trembling climax before he allowed himself the same release. Clint groaned with pleasure and relief when he blasted his seed inside Ellie's love chamber.

"This is the first time I have made love by choice," Ellie sighed.

"It can be one of the best experiences you'll ever know," the Gunsmith assured her.

"I have heard that in the past," the girl said, snuggling against Clint's bare chest. "But until now, I did not know what joy love could bring."

Ellie's remark made Clint uneasy.

"Well, making love isn't the same as being in love," he told her.

"Sex without love is rape, yes?" Ellie declared. "And we made love by choice. This makes the cause of our coupling clear. Doesn't it?"

"Oh, no," the Gunsmith rasped through his teeth.

The roar of a shotgun echoed through the night. The sound rode up from the street to the open window of Clint's room. Ellie squealed when the Gunsmith abruptly withdrew from her. He snatched the modified Colt forty-five from its holster and dashed to the window.

Under the circumstances, Clint was almost grateful for the interruption. Whatever threat might wait outside, it didn't worry the Gunsmith as much as Ellie Dove. Clint knew how to fight men with guns, but a possessive girl with romantic notions was something he didn't care to tangle with.

FOUR

Still naked, the Gunsmith peered out the window into the street below, but he could see little more than shadows. A woman screamed and a man shouted. Clint ignored their voices and continued to scan the area for a solid clue.

Clint realized the sound of the shotgun had been much closer than the voices of the startled citizens. He searched the surrounding shadows until he noticed movement in an alley between the sheriff's office and the general store. The shapes of two men stirred in the darkness. Clint recognized the long slender cylinders of rifle barrels jutting from the humanoid shadows like devil's horns.

"What is it?" Ellie asked fearfully.

"I don't know yet," Clint replied.

"Maybe it's just a drunken cowboy letting off some steam," the girl suggested, although her tone contained more hopeful expectation than conviction.

"I don't think so," the Gunsmith said. "Get my clothes, will you? I don't want to go out there buck naked."

"Why are you leaving?" she asked.

"To find out what those fellas are hiding in the alley for," Clint answered, pointing at the sinister figures he'd spotted in the dark.

"But they might be the Waldrens," Ellie gasped.

"That's why I've gotta check on them," he told her. "Now are you going to get my clothes or not?"

"No," she said sharply.

"Have it your way, lady," Clint growled as he hurried to the side of the bed and gathered up his clothes.

"No, you can't go out there," Ellie insisted.

"Like hell I can't," he replied gruffly, pulling on his trousers. "Calhune might need help. Besides, who the fuck do you think you are to give me orders?"

His language startled Ellie so completely she couldn't reply for several seconds—which was exactly why Clint had cursed at her.

"What about me?" she finally asked. "Don't you care about me?"

"You'll be safe if you just stay put," Clint told her as he slid into his shirt. "We can't say the same about Sheriff Calhune."

He pulled on his boots and grabbed the gunbelt from the headboard. Then Clint bolted from the room. He bounded down the stairway, taking three steps with each leaping stride. The Gunsmith ran past Joel Cabot at the front desk and crossed the lobby to the front door.

Clint peeled back the window shade and gazed outside. Another shot erupted and a tongue of flame streaked from the shadows between the sheriff's office and the general store. The Gunsmith recognized the crack of a medium caliber rifle.

He heard a man's yelp from the opposite end of town. It was a cry of alarm, not pain. Clint guessed someone had ventured into the street and a gunman had fired a shot just to discourage the curious.

But what if they decide the best way to discourage a

fella is to kill him? Clint thought.

"Uh . . . Mr. Adams?" Cabot called softly. "Do you have a plan about what to do about this?"

"I'm not even sure what 'this' is all about yet," Clint replied. "But I figure the safest way to find out isn't by going through this door. Where's the other exit?"

"I'll show you, sir." Cabot escorted Clint to a storage room behind his desk. Cabot pointed at a door with one hand while he fished in his pocket with the other.

"This leads to an alley," the clerk explained, extracting a key from his pocket. "It's between the hotel and the bank."

"Okay," Clint began. "Let me out. Then lock the door and don't open it unless you're real sure you can trust whoever might come rapping on it. And don't trust any of the Waldrens no matter what crazy story they tell you."

"I understand, sir," Cabot agreed as he unlocked the door.

"And you'd better get your gun," Clint advised. "Just in case."

The Gunsmith opened the door and stepped into the dark alley beyond. No sooner had he emerged than he saw the outline of a man stationed at the mouth of the alley. The figure whirled and swung a rifle toward Clint.

The Gunsmith reacted instantly. He dropped to one knee and pressed his body against the doorjamb for cover. The enemy gunman's rifle roared. Clint heard the lead projectile smash into the open door. Wood cracked from the impact.

The muzzle flash flooded the alley with a brief burst

of brilliant orange light. Clint saw his opponent's face beneath the shapeless brim of a ten-gallon hat. The man's features were hard, with a hawkbill nose and cold gray eyes. His lips were curled back in a snarl which bared tobacco-stained teeth.

The Gunsmith saw all this even as he aimed his Colt revolver at the gunman and squeezed the trigger. A 230-grain slug slammed into the rifleman's chest. The man cried out as his body was hurtled backward by the force of the bullet. He fell across the threshold of the alley and tumbled into the street.

"Holy Jesus!" a voice shouted. "Pa! Pa! They done shot Zeke! Looks to be they purely shot 'im dead too!"

"Go get them murderin' bastards!" another voice bellowed. "Ain't nobody what guns down a Waldren and lives to brag 'bout what he done!"

Any doubt Clint had concerning the identity of his assailants was gone now. The Waldrens had come down from their mountain to get Ellie. Obviously, they had to be dog-crazy to go up against an entire town just to reclaim their illegal slave girl.

The Waldrens might be short on good sense, but they still had plenty of determination and dumb courage to pull such a lunatic stunt. Clint didn't find this very comforting. Crazy men are notoriously unpredictable and will take chances no sane man would even consider. Clint hoped the Waldrens proved to be as rash as they were daring.

Two rifle shots exploded from the alley by the sheriff's office. Bullets smacked into the wall of the bank near Clint. He ducked automatically although neither missile came within a yard of him. Clint heard one of the slugs whine when it ricocheted off brick.

Trying to pin me down, he thought. *That means*

there's probably at least one of them coming for me from another direction . . .

He moved to the far end of the alley and waited in the densest shadows. Another shot erupted and a bullet struck the ground near Clint's feet. Dirt spat up at him and he cursed under his breath.

Clint wondered if he'd somehow made himself a better target when he changed position. He glanced up at the sky to see if the moon illuminated his present hiding place.

The figure of a rifle-toting assailant leaned over the edge of the hotel roof. Clint immediately raised his pistol and triggered it twice. The gunman dropped his weapon; the rifle clattered to the ground.

Clint saw the would-be assassin clamp both hands to his bullet-shattered face before he toppled off the roof. The man's body crashed to earth like a bag of grain.

"Jethro?" a voice called out. "You get that son of a bitch, boy?"

"Pa!" Clint shouted back. "I'm hurt, Pa! Hurt pretty bad!"

"Jed Boy is a-comin', son," Waldren's voice assured him. "Did you kill that bastard, Jethro?"

"Yeah," the Gunsmith replied. "I done killed 'im good and dead, Pa. . . ."

"Goddamn it!" Waldren bellowed. "You ain't Jethro! Jed Boy, watch yourself! Best get back here quick as a rabbit. Hear?"

The Gunsmith gathered up the rifle Jethro had dropped. He dusted it off and checked it as best he could in the poor light. It was a .44-caliber lever-action Winchester and it seemed to be in good condition.

Clint favored a pistol to a long gun. When he needed the extra range of a rifle, he preferred his own

Springfield carbine. He didn't like betting his life on a weapon he wasn't familiar with.

Clint carried the Winchester to the mouth of the alley and adopted a prone stance. He held the rifle in his left fist and pointed the Colt at the shadows between the sheriff's office and the general store. Clint aimed high and fired a round into the night sky.

The Gunsmith immediately rolled to the right and braced the buttstock of the Winchester to his shoulder. The gunman across the street opened fire. Dirt burst from the ground where Clint had been only a second before.

Clint's attention was on the muzzle-flash of his unseen opponent. He snap aimed, worked the Winchester lever to jack a round into the breech and squeezed the trigger. A scream of agony told him the enemy gunman hadn't succeeded in changing position as Clint had done.

Suddenly, a figure swung into the mouth of the alley. A pair of mud-splattered boots nearly stomped on the barrel of the Gunsmith's rifle. Clint gasped in surprise as he started to roll away from the invader who towered above him.

The gunman didn't notice Clint at first. He was too busy pumping lead into the alley. The man blindly fired a revolver at the shadows. The Waldren gunhawk held the pistol in one hand and fanned the hammer with the other. This allowed him to fire the single-action revolver with enormous speed but zero accuracy. Bullets slammed into walls and sizzled into the night. Clint doubted that any of the slugs would have struck him if he had been standing right in the middle of the alley in front of the idiot.

"You demon-seed puke-eater!" Jed Boy shrieked. "You killed my Pa!"

Clint suddenly propped himself up with his left hand and lashed out with the Winchester. The steel barrel struck Jed Boy's wrist. Bone snapped and the kid's pistol fell from numb fingers.

The Gunsmith quickly chopped the rifle barrel across the side of Jed Boy's knee. The youth howled in pain and fell to all fours. He screamed again when his right hand touched the ground and the broken wrist protested the sudden strain. The kid rolled over on his back, clutching the shattered wrist in his left hand as he sobbed hopelessly.

Clint rose and walked to the disabled youth. Then he clipped Jed Boy under the chin with the walnut stock of the Winchester. The kid sighed as if grateful to be rendered unconscious.

"Good night, Jed Boy," the Gunsmith muttered.

FIVE

The townsfolk found Sheriff Calhune bound and gagged in the alley beside his office. The lawman had been attacked by two of the Waldrens while making his rounds.

"I managed to fire my shotgun before one of them hit me over the head," the sheriff explained as he sat behind his desk in the law office. "Don't know how long I was out cold. When I came to, I was all tied up with a dirty rag stuffed in my mouth. Lucky they didn't find it so easy to take you, Clint."

"Maybe they would have if you hadn't managed to fire that warning shot," the Gunsmith replied, trying to help the lawman save face. "How's your head?"

"Nothing a couple shots of whiskey won't cure," Calhune replied. "Care to join me?"

"Sure." Clint grinned.

"You kill all the Waldrens except the kid?" Calhune inquired, tilting his head at the jail cell where Jed Boy was held prisoner.

"The old man is still alive," Clint replied. "Caught a bullet in the upper chest. The doctor is trying to patch him up, but I don't think he'll live to see the dawn. The doc seems to feel the same way."

"Can't say as that'll break my heart," Calhune

admitted. He opened a desk drawer and removed two glasses and a bottle of red-eye. "Reckon Ellie's safe enough now. No more need to worry about the Waldrens, that's for sure."

"But do I have to worry about Ellie?" Clint muttered to himself.

"What's that?" the sheriff asked.

"Nothing." Clint shrugged. "Just thinking out loud. Wondering what you want to do about Ellie now."

"Any reason why she can't just stay in your room until tomorrow?" Calhune asked.

"I've got to be moving on in the morning, Sheriff," Clint explained. "And I'm not taking her with me."

"I already understood that, Clint," Calhune replied.

"You understand and I understand," the Gunsmith stated. "I just hope Ellie will too."

"I won't be leaving with you in the morning," Ellie Dove told Clint when he finally returned to the hotel room.

"Oh?" the Gunsmith replied, startled that his problem seemed to have worked itself out.

"It wouldn't work with us, Clint," she announced. "You are a very good man, but not the sort of man I want to marry."

"I see," Clint nodded.

"No, I don't think you do," Ellie continued. "I'm a Christian. Perhaps not a good Christian, but I still want my children to be raised as good Christians. I want them to go to school and attend church. I want them to learn how to read and write and to know the Bible from cover to cover."

"And you don't figure I've got enough Christian in me." The Gunsmith smiled. "Well, I reckon you might be right about that, Ellie."

"I don't mean to be spiteful," the girl said stiffly. "You've helped me and I am thankful for all you've done."

"Don't mention it," the Gunsmith urged. "You're right about one thing, Ellie. I'm not the right fella for you to think about getting married to. I wouldn't be a fit husband for you, or anybody else."

"Perhaps one day you'll change, Clint." Ellie smiled.

SIX

Clint Adams left Holden the following morning. Sheriff Calhune watched the Gunsmith's wagon roll out of town with Duke tied to the rear of the rig. The lawman felt he owed a debt to the Gunsmith and now it seemed unlikely he'd ever be able to repay it.

Doctor Wells arrived at Calhune's office shortly after noon that same day looking as if he had worked all night without taking time to blink. In fact, that's exactly what he'd done.

"Old Jed Waldren died half an hour ago," Wells told Calhune. "I got the bullet out, but it had crushed Jed's manubrium, the bone just above the sternum. Pieces of it caused internal bleeding. Nothing I could do about it."

"You tried, Doc," Calhune assured him.

"Yeah." Wells sighed. "Reckon when the Gunsmith sets out to kill a fella, it's just a matter of time before he gets his wish."

"What do you figure Clint should have done when the Waldrens were shooting at him?" the sheriff asked crossly.

"Hell, Luke," the doctor began, surprised by Calhune's defensive reaction, "I wouldn't think you'd have much good to say about a gunfighting drifter like Clint Adams."

"Clint isn't a gunfighter," Calhune declared. "He didn't cause any trouble in Holden. The Waldrens did. Clint probably saved my life last night. Maybe saved a lot of other folks too. Hard to say how many people might have been killed if the Waldrens hadn't been stopped once and for all."

"Okay, Luke," Wells said, holding up his hands. "I see your point. Reckon I wasn't being too objective after spending all night trying to keep Old Man Waldren alive."

"Maybe I was a bit short-tempered myself, Doc."

"While I'm here," Wells began, "maybe I should check on the kid. I put those splints on in sort of a hurry last night. Wouldn't hurt for me to make sure everything is set right for the bones to knit properly."

"Sure, Doc," Calhune replied. "I'll open Jed Boy's cell and you can—"

"Sheriff," Tom Goddard, a stocky muscle-bound young man who worked as the local blacksmith called as he entered the office. "There's a fella over at the saloon been askin' questions about the Gunsmith."

"What do you mean, Tom?" Calhune frowned.

"Well, there's a big guy with a limp and a funny accent who wants to know why Adams was here and where he's headin' next."

"Maybe he's a friend of Clint's," Doc Wells suggested.

"Maybe," the lawman said without conviction. "But I figure I'd better have a talk with this stranger."

"Looks like you'll get your chance, Sheriff," Tom said as he glanced out the door. "Fella's headin' this way."

DYNAMITE JUSTICE

Calhune heard a heavy object strike the plankwalk outside. The sound rung against wood again. The sheriff wondered what the noise might be.

Then a man appeared in the doorway. Calhune had to make a conscious effort to keep his mouth from falling open when he saw the huge figure standing at the threshold of his office.

The man was at least six and a half feet tall. He wore a linen shirt, gray suit trousers and low-heeled eastern boots. Calhune noticed the right foot appeared to be almost twice the size of his left. *Clubfoot,* Calhune thought. *Maybe a wooden leg.*

Coils of muscle strained against the fabric of the stranger's clothes. Instead of a stetson he wore a blue beret. His face was hard and stiff like a mask carved of walnut wood. The man did not wear a gunbelt. He didn't need one. He carried a sawed-off shotgun hung from a shoulder strap by his right hip.

"*Bonjour,*" the big man declared as he limped into the office. His right foot slammed into the floorboards forcibly with each step.

"Can I help you, mister?" Calhune asked, rising from his chair.

"I hope so, *oui,*" the enormous Frenchman nodded. "I would like to know about Clint Adams. The man known as *l'Armurier*—the Gunsmith."

"What do you want to know about him, fella?" the sheriff inquired.

"I understand he was in Holden until early this morning," the giant replied. "Did he say where he was going or if he would return to this town later?"

"Why do you want to know?" Calhune demanded.

"I have my reasons," the Frenchman said simply.

"You'd better tell me what they are if you expect

any answers," the lawman told him.

"Clint Adams is a friend," the big man stated.

"Is that a fact?" Calhune sneered. "For some reason I don't believe you, fella. Who are you anyway?"

The Frenchman shrugged. "My name is not important."

"Then why are you afraid to tell it to me?" the sheriff asked.

"We have nothing more to say to one another, *monsieur*," the huge man said as he turned to leave.

"You hold on a minute, Frenchy!" Tom Goddard snapped.

The blacksmith lunged forward and seized the stranger's arm. The Frenchman was only slightly taller than Tom and the blacksmith figured no fancy pants foreigner could match his muscle power.

Without warning, the stranger stamped the heel of his right foot into Tom's instep. The blacksmith howled in pain as bones crunched like dry twigs inside his foot. The larger man broke free of Tom's grasp and lashed the back of a fist across the blacksmith's face.

Tom Goddard half staggered and half hopped away. The stranger's right leg whipped a brutal kick to Tom's midsection. The blacksmith gasped and collapsed to the floor in a moaning lump.

"That's enough!" Calhune ordered, drawing his sidearm.

The Frenchman glanced at the sheriff's pistol and sighed. Calhune felt a cold shiver travel up his spine. The ominous stranger didn't seem the least bit concerned by the lawman's gun.

"Your friend should not have touched me, Sheriff,"

the Frenchman declared. "I acted in self-defense and I have broken no laws. You have no right to hold me. *Oui*?"

"Fella's right, Luke," Doctor Wells added as he knelt beside the fallen blacksmith. "Tom was out of line."

He began to roll Goddard over on his back when he saw a pool of scarlet on the floor.

"Jesus Christ!" Wells exclaimed. "He's vomiting blood!"

Calhune glared at the stranger. "Did you have to kick him so hard?"

"He should not have touched me," the Frenchman repeated without emotion.

The stranger limped from the office. Calhune thumbed back the hammer of his revolver. The Frenchman must have heard the triple-click of the single-action pistol, yet he did not even glance over his shoulder at the sheriff. The big man was obviously confident Calhune would not pull the trigger.

And he was right.

Calhune eased the Colt's hammer forward to uncock the weapon and shoved the gun into leather. He cursed angrily and slammed a fist on the top of his desk in frustration.

"I should have shot that bastard," he muttered.

"In the back?" Wells shook his head even as he gingerly probed Tom Goddard's torso with his fingertips. "You couldn't do that, Luke. You're not a murderer."

"But the Frenchman is," Calhune said grimly. "That son of a bitch is a cold-blooded killer."

"Come on, Luke," the doctor began as he took

Tom's pulse. "He didn't use his shotgun, did he? A man doesn't kick somebody in the stomach if he intends to kill him."

"I'm not sure what he intended to do to Tom," Calhune said. "But I'm sure he plans to kill Clint."

"My God," Wells whispered. "Tom's dead!"

"What?" Calhune stared at the doctor. "Are you sure?"

"Of course I'm sure," Wells snapped.

"But Tom was built like an oak tree," the sheriff stated. "How could one kick kill him?"

"I don't understand it myself, Luke," the doctor admitted as he used two fingers to press Tom's eyelids shut. "There's a purple bruise at Tom's solar plexus. All I can figure is the kick must've ruptured his heart. Stopped it as sure as a bullet."

"Christ," Calhune rasped. "Nobody can hit that hard."

"The Frenchman can," Wells corrected. "He just did it, by God."

"And he's going after Clint," the sheriff added grimly.

"I hope the Gunsmith kills that French butcher," Wells confessed. "Whoever the bastard is."

"If he doesn't, I reckon Clint will wind up the same as poor Tom here."

SEVEN

"I hope this map is right," Clint Adams muttered as he unfolded a sheet of paper.

He checked the chart once more. It indicated the dirt road which Clint traveled, but it also suggested that the nearest mountains were several miles away, yet he rode the wagon within a hundred yards of a column of stony monoliths.

Clint pulled up the reins, then reached into a saddlebag by the driver's seat and extracted a Dolland—a collapsible telescope favored by seafaring men. At the rear of the wagon, Duke whinnied loudly.

"What's the matter, big fella?" Clint called back to his prized black gelding. "You mad because I didn't yell 'whoa' before I stopped the rig? Don't tell me you rammed your snout into the back of the wagon."

Duke whinnied again and pawed the ground. The Gunsmith pulled the Dolland to full length and raised it to his eye. He scanned over the peaks of the surrounding mountains. In the distance, he saw the pinnacles of several much taller mountains.

"Those must be the ones on the map," Clint commented. "I guess little mountains don't count in Colorado."

Duke whinnied louder and rose up on his hind legs to

tug at the guideline attached to the wagon. The gelding wasn't just upset. Duke was trying to warn Clint of danger.

The Gunsmith recognized Duke's warning. Long ago he had learned to respect the horse's keen senses and intelligent judgment. Clint believed Duke could smell a mud hole in the desert a mile before he reached it, and that he could hear a baby rat pissing on cotton.

Clint had faith in Duke's opinion. If the horse figured there was danger, then the Gunsmith had better prepare for trouble—pronto. He jumped down from the wagon and reached for his Springfield carbine under the driver's seat.

Wood splintered from the bench when a large caliber bullet smashed into it. Clint heard the report of a rifle as he grabbed the Springfield and pulled it free. The Gunsmith's heart raced as he crouched behind the wagon. The horses whinnied with fear, but the animals had been trained to overcome their natural gun-shyness. They wouldn't run off unless Clint ordered them to.

The Gunsmith realized that the time lapse between when the bullet had struck and the sound of the sniper's rifle suggested his opponent was still some distance away. Whoever it might be, he was obviously armed with a big-bore, long-range weapon. Probably a fifty-caliber Sharps buffalo rifle, Clint suspected.

Another gunshot snarled and a slug smacked into the frame of the wagon just above Clint's head. He threw himself to the ground and rolled away from the rig. A bullet kicked dirt from the ground, narrowly missing Clint's tumbling form.

There was more than one sniper. The second gunman was stationed on the opposite side of the ravine. He also appeared to be closer than his partner. Clint figured the second sniper was armed with a lever-action weapon due to the speed of the two shots fired from that direction.

Clint leaped to his feet and dashed to the closest cover—a pile of rock rubble at the base of the nearest mountain. A large lead missile whined against a boulder. Clint heard the bellow of the first sniper's weapon as he scrambled behind the stony shelter.

Bastards set up a crossfire ambush, Clint thought. *Pretty clever. They've got me boxed up now. Any way I move I'll have to expose myself to one of them.*

The Gunsmith didn't waste time wondering who the ambushers might be or why they'd attacked him. Clint Adams had enemies he didn't even know about. The snipers could be old foes from the past or trigger-happy gunhawks trying to acquire a reputation by killing the Gunsmith.

However, the most likely possibility was that the pair were simply highwaymen. It's safer to say "stand and deliver" to a corpse than someone who could shoot back. Drygulchers like to minimize their risks, and many of them were willing to murder a total stranger just for whatever money the fellow might have in his pocket.

The only fact that interested the Gunsmith at the moment was that they were trying to kill him. Only one question was on his mind: *How do I survive?*

Clint had one surprise ace up his sleeve. He still held the Dolland in his left hand. The Gunsmith used the telescope to once again scan the rock walls. The powerful lenses magnified his view of the stone surface. Clint examined the rugged face of the mountain. It seemed void of life, but boulders don't fire rifles. . . .

Then Clint located the sniper. The gunman was crouching by a large round rock. He was a young man clad in denim trousers and a checkered shirt. The face beneath a tan stetson didn't seem familiar to the Gunsmith. Probably just a cowboy turned drygulcher.

As the Gunsmith suspected the sniper was armed with a Sharps Big Fifty, a powerful, single-shot, breech-loading rifle with an impressive range. Accurate shooting at greater than fifteen hundred yards isn't unknown for a sharpshooter with a Big Fifty. And the cowboy was stationed much closer than that. Clint estimated the sniper was only about three hundred yards away, beyond the accurate range of the Gunsmith's Springfield.

Clint decided to give the sniper a surprise. He aimed the Springfield like a motor, pointing it at the peak of the mountain. Clint aimed high and hoped the bullet would descend in an arch to strike near the sniper's position. The principle worked with field artillery, but the Gunsmith didn't know if it would apply to a rifle round. He'd find out.

The Gunsmith squeezed the trigger.

He grabbed his Dolland and quickly trained it on the killer's position. The man had retreated behind the closest boulder. Clint caught a glimpse of the gunman's startled face. It was impossible to say how close the Springfield bullet had come, but it had succeeded in convincing the drygulcher to seek cover.

The Gunsmith bolted from his own shelter and scrambled to another boulder. The second gunman didn't open fire. This suggested the sniper wasn't in position to get a clear shot at Clint. The Gunsmith guessed that the killer wasn't at a proper angle to even see him. At least, he hoped that was the case.

DYNAMITE JUSTICE

A shot bellowed and a big lead missile smacked into the first boulder Clint had used for cover. The Gunsmith smiled as he crouched behind his new shelter. The guy with the Sharps didn't realize Clint had changed his position.

The Gunsmith waited.

A trio of rifle rounds pelted the first boulder. Clint realized the sniper with the lever-action weapon must have attacked his old position as well. Neither killer suspected Clint had moved to new cover.

The snipers' tactic was simple enough. The guy with the repeater was trying to get Clint to break cover and expose himself to the Sharps rifleman. Not a bad plan, except they were still concentrating on the wrong position. Clint carefully peered around the edge of his shelter.

He saw the gunman with the Sharps climb down the face of the mountain opposite his position. The Gunsmith had hoped the snipers would get impatient and decide to draw closer. They probably thought Clint may have been shot, or they hoped he'd be a better target if they moved in. Clint aimed his Springfield. The front sight bisected the ambusher's checkered shirt. He squeezed the trigger.

A forty-five caliber bullet punched into the sniper's chest. It drilled through his heart and kicked the man's body backward against the rock wall. The sniper tumbled forward and plunged headfirst to the ground fifty feet below.

"Goddamn!" a voice snarled.

Clint retreated behind the boulder. He hadn't acted a split second too soon. A rifle bullet chipped stone inches from his head. The second gunman blasted two more rounds at Clint's position. The Gunsmith cried out in mock agony and tossed his Springfield into the open—in clear view of his opponent.

The Gunsmith remained behind the boulder and drew the modified double-action Colt from leather. Once again he waited. Playing possum is an old trick, but old tricks still work. If the sniper was a careless amateur, he'd probably be suckered by the tactic. Otherwise, Clint would have to be ready for some tricks from his enemy as well.

Suddenly, a shadow fell across the Gunsmith. He instinctively rolled to the right. The report of a rifle roared above him.

Clint glanced up at the figure which stood on top of the boulder. He snap-aimed the Colt and triggered two rapid double-action rounds. The gunman's body twisted violently like a fish tossed on a hot surface. A Henry repeater tumbled from his fingers before he fell to the sand in a twitching, dying heap.

The Gunsmith scrambled back to cover and cautiously gazed about for any back-up gunmen who might be waiting for him. He doubted this was the case, but he was too experienced in the art of surviving a firefight to take any chances. When Clint was reasonably sure it was safe, he approached the body of Sniper Number Two. Clint examined the man's face. Another stranger.

"Wonder what this was all about," he commented as he nudged the dead man's head with the toe of a boot. "But I reckon it would be too much to expect any answers from either of you guys now."

EIGHT

Dublin appeared to be a small, quiet town. The collection of houses with tar-patched roofs and tin chimney pipes resembled pictures of a European hamlet more than a frontier community in the American West. The Gunsmith sighed with disappointment. Dublin didn't look like it would have a large enough population to make his trip worthwhile.

As Clint entered town he noticed several figures darting about and heard the confused chatter of numerous voices expressing alarm and surprise, issuing orders. Clint continued to drive his wagon into the town although he heard Duke whinny a familiar warning once more.

"Oh, shit," the Gunsmith muttered. "Not again."

Half a dozen armed men marched toward the wagon. They were dressed in canvas overalls and cotton shirts with caps and derbies for headgear. None of them wore a gunbelt. Most were armed with rifles or shotguns. Their hostile, suspicious faces warned that they wouldn't hesitate to use their weapons.

"Hold it right there, mate," ordered a short wiry man with a ferret face, a bushy mustache and a saddle gun. "Unless you'd be in a hurry to find out if there be life after death."

The Gunsmith had already brought the wagon to a halt. He raised his hands to shoulder level to show that he offered them no threat.

"You fellas always so friendly?" Clint inquired.

"We'll ask the questions, mister," a large muscular character snapped. His eyes resembled two cobalt flames set in a wide, hard face. "We're not of a mind to be listenin' to any sass from you, so you best watch your tongue."

"O'Quinn!" a deep, authoritative voice called out. "Don't threaten the man. He stopped his rig for us, didn't he?"

The crowd parted to make a path for a man who strode toward the Gunsmith. He was average height with a muscular upper torso and a slender waist. His rust-colored hair was gray at the temples and his lantern-jawed face was a mask of Irish determination.

What interested Clint most about the man was his catlike stride and confident gestures. He was a man accustomed to commanding others. Clint also noticed he was the only one in the crowd with a handgun. He carried a pistol thrust in his belt in a cross-draw position. The Gunsmith recognized the weapon. It was a forty-five caliber British Tranter revolver.

"Are you in charge, friend?" Clint inquired.

"In charge?" The Irishman raised an eyebrow. "Not really. I'm just a civic leader of sorts. And don't call me a friend until you can be provin' you mean it."

"What should I call you instead?" the Gunsmith asked.

"Name's Corrigan," the Irishman replied. "Jack Corrigan. As for this little town, we call it Dublin. It's a bit of Ireland planted here in the United States."

"So I've heard," Clint remarked.

"All the introductions have been a bit one-sided so

far," Corrigan stated. "Who are you and what's your reason for comin' here?"

"My name is Clint Adams and I make my living as a traveling gunsmith. I ride around in this wagon and fix people's firearms. When I heard about Dublin, I figured I might be able to get some business here."

"Maybe my gun doesn't work at that." O'Quinn, the big surly man, sneered as he aimed his Winchester at the Gunsmith's face. "Would you like me to pull this trigger so we can find out?"

"Be careful with that bloody thing, O'Quinn," Corrigan snapped. "We don't want to be killin' Mr. Adams by accident, now do we?"

"I should hope not," the Gunsmith muttered.

"Should we take a look inside his wagon, Jack?" the wiry little gunman inquired.

Corrigan nodded. "Aye. You and O'Quinn keep an eye on Adams, Durkan. The rest of us will check out his rig."

"Maybe O'Quinn and Durkan be willin' to take orders from you," an elderly man with a pair of wire-rimmed glasses perched on the bridge of his slender nose began, "but you not be in charge here, Jack Corrigan."

"Then why don't you go find O'Hara and bring him here, Duffy?" Corrigan asked sharply. "If he's supposed to be a leader, then O'Hara should damn well be here and make some decisions, by God."

"I'm here, Corrigan!" a voice announced curtly. "So you and your mates can just relax a bit."

A stocky figure strode forward. He was thickly built with a balding pate. In contrast, his jaw was covered by a dense iron-gray beard. The man walked with a shillelagh cane, although he did not appear to be lame.

"We'll relax when we're sure about this Adams

fella," the diminutive Durkan replied.

"Haven't you blokes ever heard of Clint Adams," O'Hara demanded. "Maybe you'll recall his moniker instead. He's known as the Gunsmith."

"Jesus, Mary and Joseph!" old Duffy exclaimed. "You mean he's that gunfighter fella?"

"Why didn't you tell us you're the Gunsmith?" O'Quinn growled.

"I told you fellas I'm *a* gunsmith by trade," Clint answered. "But I never asked for that silly handle and I never call myself by it."

"What brings you to Dublin, Mr. Adams?" O'Hara asked.

"Says he's lookin' for business as a traveling gunsmith," Durkan began.

"Sure'n Mr. Adams can talk for himself," O'Hara said sternly.

"Look," Clint began. "I'm not stupid enough to reach for my gun and try to shoot it out with all of you guys. How about letting me lower my hands?"

"Go ahead." O'Hara nodded. "But answer my question."

"Well, I headed this way to see about making a profit with my gunsmith business," Clint said. "But I think I'll just move on to a more friendly town."

"Or report back to Huntington-Smythe," the burly O'Quinn sneered. "Who else would hire the likes of the Gunsmith?"

"I don't have to report to anybody," Clint said. "I'm self-employed. Besides, I never heard of this Smythe character."

"He's the reason we're armed to the teeth and ready for trouble," O'Hara explained. "Bit of a feud between his people and us."

"Feud?" Clint raised his eyebrows.

"Not your concern, Adams," Corrigan said. "If you be tellin' us the truth and you're not involved already."

"Mr. Adams deserves an explanation," O'Hara insisted. "Huntington-Smythe is our enemy. He's been harassing us ever since we built this town a couple months ago. We've no intention of knuckling under to that English warlord, I'll tell you that."

"Would this harassment include trying to cut off supplies coming into town?" Clint inquired.

"That's right," O'Hara confirmed. "Did his boys try to stop you on your way here? We heard gunshots and wondered what might be afoot."

"A foot is that odd looking thing at the end of your leg." Clint smiled. "The one with the toes on it."

"Very funny, Adams," Durkan growled. "Now, did you have any trouble on the trail or not?"

"Nothing I couldn't handle," the Gunsmith replied. "But I think Huntington-Smythe lost a couple of his boys today."

"Did you kill them?" Corrigan asked with interest.

"They didn't leave me any choice," Clint told him. "I took their wallets for identification. Only one guy had his name in his wallet. Have to guess about the other fella for now. Buried them both back in the ravine where they attacked me. If you want to take a look, you'll find them under a pair of rock mounds."

"In that case, Mr. Adams"—Corrigan smiled—"might I be buyin' you a drink, sir?"

"Maybe later," Clint replied. "Right now, I'd like some more information."

"Then come along with me," O'Hara invited.

NINE

"Sorry about the unfriendly reception, Mr. Adams," O'Hara began as he escorted the Gunsmith into his cabin. "Not very good Irish hospitality."

"Just call me Clint," the Gunsmith told him. "I can understand why you folks have to be sort of careful, but Corrigan and his pals seemed a little too eager to find an excuse to blast me to hell."

"They can be a bit hotheaded," O'Hara admitted as he sank into one of three chairs at a small wooden table. "Corrigan would like to be running things here, but nobody is willin' to follow him except O'Quinn and Durkan. At least, not yet."

A plump, middle-aged woman dressed in a gray gingham dress and a dirty apron entered the room. She smiled at Clint and tried to straighten her unkempt gray hair.

"Oh," she began, "I didn't know we had company, Sean."

"Aye," O'Hara replied. "Fetch some whiskey, Maureen. Our guest must be thirsty."

"Certainly, dear." The woman hurried to a cabinet and removed a brown bottle.

"You wanted some answers," O'Hara began, turning again to Clint. "Well, I'll try to explain everything best I can."

"I'm listening," Clint assured him.

"Well, I'm the mayor," the Irishman said, leaning back in his chair. "At least for now. Guess that qualifies me to answer most of your questions. Let's see, I suppose I should begin at the beginning, eh?"

Maureen placed the bottle on the table and smiled at the Gunsmith as she put two glasses beside the whiskey.

"We men have business to discuss," O'Hara told his wife. "Go see to your laundry."

"Yes, dear," the woman said. She turned and headed for the back door.

"Now, where was I?" the Irishman wondered as he yanked the cork from the bottle. "Ah, yes. I was telling you about Dublin. Well, we're all Irish immigrants as you probably guessed. We came to the United States because the British gave us hell in Ireland. We heard America was heaven on earth—complete with streets paved in bloody gold. Childish, eh?"

"That depends on how literally you take that description," Clint remarked, nodding his thanks as O'Hara poured generous drams into each glass.

"Oh, I don't expect any of us figured the cobblestones would really be shiny yellow." O'Hara sighed. "But we did hope this country wouldn't be crawling with Brits."

"I haven't noticed that we've got that many Englishmen here."

"Maybe you haven't looked," the Irishman told him. "You've got lots of them. Seems that most Americans are of English descent. Lots of people came over from Britain to seek employment here. Not surprising since this country is so bloody big. There are hundreds of Brits scattered all over America. You'd think your country and England had never fought a war."

"That was more than a century ago, Mr. O'Hara," Clint commented. "Guess we Americans are a forgiving people. Reckon the British are, too."

"Be that as it may," O'Hara muttered, "we Irish have found America to be something of a disappointment. Too many English and Welsh in the East. Not much opportunity available to us there, so we headed west. That's why we founded Dublin, Colorado. We figure maybe we could finally start over again here."

"And how has Huntington-Smythe stopped you?"

"Typical British arrogance," O'Hara answered as he quaffed a shot of whiskey. "Bastard runs a mining company less than a mile from here."

"What's he digging for?" Clint asked. "I didn't think there was much gold or silver left in Colorado."

"Simpler than that," the Irishman stated. "He's just mining for coal. Plain old bloody coal and the Limey acts as if he was digging up diamonds. Typical Englishman. Worse than that, Huntington-Smythe is a military sort. Former army officer of some kind."

"Why would he care about Dublin?" Clint asked as he sipped his whiskey.

O'Hara shrugged. "I suppose it's just because we're Irish."

"None of your people happen to be coal miners, by any chance?" the Gunsmith inquired. "Say, back in Pennsylvania?"

"I suppose you're suggesting we're Molly Maguires, is that it?" The Irishman clucked his tongue with disgust. "I'm a potato farmer, Clint. So are most of the rest of us. Not that we don't have some sympathy for the Mollies, mind you."

"Sympathy with coal miners who have to work in wretched conditions is one thing," Clint said. "But the Molly Maguires are a different matter, Mr. O'Hara."

"Name's Sean," the Irishman told him as he poured himself another drink. "Maybe you don't realize that the Mollies were formed to fight those lousy conditions and to protest the rotten wages Irish miners earn under those tinhorn tyrants who own the coal companies."

"The way I hear it," Clint began, "the Molly Maguires started in Ireland, not Pennsylvania. Wasn't Molly Maguire some kind of Irish martyr? Later a secret society was formed to combat the British. They adopted the woman-warrior's name and used to disguise themselves by dressing up in women's clothing."

"You surprise me, Clint," the mayor admitted.

"Well, I've never heard of the Mollies wearing dresses in the United States," the Gunsmith added. "They usually wear sacks over their heads in Pennsylvania. Of course, what kind of disguise the Mollies want to use isn't as important as their brand of tactics. Beating people up, destroying property and murder isn't exactly an admirable form of protest."

"Don't talk about things you don't understand," O'Hara advised. "There's no other way they get attention about the mines. The politicians don't care. Bloody mine owners are usually British and the police are mostly Welsh. Maybe violence is the only method left to them."

"I'm well aware that there are circumstances when violence is the only logical resort," Clint assured him.

"But I'm not so sure the Mollies are in that position. One thing is pretty certain. Most of the victims of Molly Maguire violence haven't been directly responsible for the conditions of the mines. Most have simply been critics of Molly tactics. I don't think because somebody disagrees with you that gives you a right to kill him."

"Sorry we got on this subject." O'Hara sighed. "Not really important since no one in Dublin is in with the Molly Maguires."

"But maybe Huntington-Smythe figures you are," the Gunsmith suggested.

"Don't tell me you approve of what he's done?" the Irishman snapped.

"How can I when I still don't know what the hell is going on?"

"Very well," O'Hara growled. "That Limey bastard accused us of sabotaging his bloody mine. Oh, you're probably right. I suppose he's accusing us of being Molly Maguires, but that's just an excuse to try to drive us out."

"Well," the Gunsmith began, "I'm no friend of Huntington-Smythe myself. I don't take kindly to having someone shooting at me—even if I am mistaken for somebody else. Still, I didn't get such a great reception here either."

"I've explained the reason for that," O'Hara declared, swallowing another glass of whiskey as if it was well water.

"Yeah," Clint said. "Well, I appreciate your hospitality. Please pass my thanks on to Mrs. O'Hara as well."

"You're leaving?" The Irishman frowned.

"Figure I should try to find this Huntington-Smythe fella and let him know that a couple of his boys won't show up for supper."

"Best stay clear of that blackguard," O'Hara warned.

"I can't just ride on and not report the deaths of two men I killed," the Gunsmith told him. "Their families have a right to know what happened to them. Besides, if I don't explain this to Huntington-Smythe, he'll probably figure you folks killed his men."

"We've already got plenty of problems with that man." O'Hara sighed. "Too many to be taken care of so easily. Payin' a visit to Huntington-Smythe won't help us with any of our troubles, Clint. It's more apt to give you a couple of your own."

TEN

When the Gunsmith emerged from O'Hara's house he was surprised to discover the sky had adopted the soft gray shade of twilight. So much had happened he had lost track of time. Clint headed for his wagon.

"Just a minute, Adams!" a voice called to him.

Clint turned to see Jack Corrigan approach. The burly O'Quinn and the diminutive Durkan tagged along behind him. Clint resisted an urge to place a hand on the comforting grips of his holstered Colt revolver.

"See you've been chatting with O'Hara," Corrigan remarked. "I suppose that means you've had enough to drink already."

"For a while," Clint answered.

"Course, the way the old boy likes his jug"—Corrigan smiled—"I figure he did most of the drinkin'. The Irish disease, don't you know. Can't say as I can debate that since I'm fond of a drink from time to time meself."

"You don't have to be Irish to feel that way," the Gunsmith grinned.

"But it doesn't hurt." Corrigan chuckled. "Besides, it's as good an excuse as any to crack open a bottle. Sure'n you'd be welcome to join us for a sip or two."

"No thanks," Clint replied. "I figure I'll be moving on."

"Come on, Clint," Corrigan began. "I trust it's all right if I call you by your Christian name. The lads and I would like to sort of make up for our rude and suspicious behavior when you first arrived in town."

"That's okay," Clint assured him.

"Did O'Hara tell you about Huntington-Smythe?"

Clint nodded. "He told me you folks aren't getting along with him very well."

"That's a bleeding understatement," Corrigan declared. "Can't we chat about this over a drink, Clint? I'm sure that watching O'Hara drink made you more thirsty."

"Okay, Jack. I'll have a drink with you."

"Good," Corrigan smiled. "I'll introduce you to the lads. They're good chaps, really. I know they seemed a bit nasty before, but that's because we figured you were in league with the Englishman."

"Nope," Clint assured him. "I'm strictly in league with myself."

Corrigan turned to O'Quinn and Durkan. The pair smiled with all the warmth of a couple of cracked tombstones.

"The big chap here is Mike O'Quinn," Corrigan explained. "Looks like a bloody beast, doesn't he? Well, that's pretty much what he is."

"Sod you, Jack," O'Quinn growled, but he grinned at the good-natured kidding.

"Really, Mike is a workhorse," Corrigan continued. "He can pull two full ore cars if you can find a harness big enough to fit him.

"Now this little bloke"—Corrigan gestured at the

smaller man—"is Timothy Durkan. Don't let his size fool you. He's a real scrapper and a bloody good powderman. Eh, Timmy?"

"Give me enough dynamite and I'll blow up the bleedin' world," Durkan replied with a wolfish smile.

"That's an interesting ambition," Clint mused. "You fellas sound like you may have done some coal mining back in Pennsylvania."

"Damn right we did," Corrigan admitted. "The three of us are bound to go to Heaven after spending two and a half years diggin' in Hell. Come along and we'll have that drink."

The trio escorted Clint to another cabin. Inside, it was evident that the place was a tavern. The furniture consisted of three tables and several chairs. There was also a crude bar made of apple crates with two long planks nailed on top.

"Welcome to the Glenmalure," Corrigan declared cheerfully. "It's the only pub in town. You won't often find this place empty."

"You own this saloon?" Clint asked as he followed the trio to the bar.

"Aye," Durkan replied. "The three of us run the place."

"I wouldn't think this town would be large enough for you fellas to make much of a profit," Clint remarked.

"Remember Dublin is an *Irish* town." Corrigan chuckled as he slipped behind the bar and reached under the counter. "Actually, we just do this as a sideline. The three of us share the work and take turns as bartender. Not a bad system. Eh, lads?"

"Jack's idea, of course," Durkan added. "He's

always comin' up with bloody brilliant plans. If'n there's ever to be an Irish governor of any state in America, that bloke will be Jack Corrigan."

"Bloody genius," O'Quinn agreed.

"What do you guys do for a living when you aren't taking care of this saloon?" the Gunsmith asked.

"Well," Corrigan began as he placed a bottle and four glasses on the counter, "we're still not too sure about that. I'm a carpenter, O'Quinn is my apprentice and Durkan is the demolitions expert. That makes us a damn good construction team. Most of our experience has been in coal mines back in Pennsylvania. Not easy to build a mineshaft and put in those ore car rails, I can tell you that."

"I believe you," Clint assured him, sipping his drink. "Did you fellas build this town?"

"Most of the buildings are our work, aye," O'Quinn said proudly.

"Nice work," Clint told him. "O'Hara tells me most of you folks are potato farmers."

"About half." Corrigan shrugged. "The rest are former dockworkers, cobblers, coal miners and other folk who got a sorry deal back East."

"This seems like an odd place for a town," Clint mused.

"Not really," Corrigan explained, placing a box of cigars on the bar. "There's good soil in the area. The large cattle ranches shouldn't mind us much and everybody is willing to work."

"The coal mines nearby seemed like an advantage when we picked this location," Durkan commented. "We figured maybe we could get work there. Not that we were eager to go back to the mines, but we could use the money. Right?"

"But that British bastard wasn't about to hire Irishmen to work his bloody mines," O'Quinn muttered.

"So, you tried to get employment from Huntington-Smythe?" Clint asked, accepting a cigar.

"Aye," Durkan answered. "But he'd rather train kids without experience and risk their lives workin' in the mines than hire us."

"Proved to be a mistake to let the Limey know about Dublin—or us." Corrigan sighed. "Didn't take long before the harassment started."

"I'll talk to Huntington-Smythe. Plan to see him anyway about his men using me for target practice."

"You're not plannin' on paying Huntington-Smythe a visit tonight, are you, Clint?" Corrigan asked.

"Why not?"

"Cause his men might blow your ruddy head off before you get a chance to tell 'em why you're there." Durkan supplied the answer.

"Best wait till morning, Clint," Corrigan advised.

"Yeah," the Gunsmith agreed. "No sense inviting trouble from a jumpy sentry who might start shooting at shadows."

"You could check in with the Widow Malloy," Corrigan suggested. "She's got a couple spare rooms that she plans to rent out. Could use the money, I reckon."

"Thanks for the suggestion." The Gunsmith nodded. "And the drink."

"Our pleasure," Corrigan assured him. "And when you see Huntington-Smythe, you might tell the bastard that we Irish be a stubborn lot. We're not about to turn tail and run. If'n it be a fight he wants, we'll surely give him one."

ELEVEN

Outside the Glenmalure, Corrigan pointed the way to the widow's boardinghouse. Clint made a mental note of its location and thanked the Irishman. Then he headed back to his wagon to take care of his horses and rig.

The Gunsmith rode the wagon to the local livery stable. Duffy, the old man, greeted Clint at the entrance. He examined the rig with interest as Clint climbed down from the driver's seat.

"Need to have your wagon and beasties looked after, eh?" Duffy remarked.

"That's right," Clint confirmed.

"No problem with that," Duffy stated. "Got two open stalls for your team."

"What about Duke?" Clint asked.

"Duke?" The old man frowned. "Oh, I see the legs of another horse tied to the back of your rig . . ."

Duffy moved to the rear of the wagon and stopped suddenly when he saw the magnificent black Arabian. The hostler stared at the horse and gasped in stunned admiration.

"Jesus Lord," he whispered. "Now that's an animal worth a bleedin' kingdom."

"He's worth a lot to me," the Gunsmith admitted.

"And I'll pay extra to make certain he gets special treatment."

"No need to fear." Duffy smiled. "I'll treat your steed like he was my own. Lord knows I wish I could own such a fine animal, but I could never be affording such a horse. I suppose there would be little point to it now since I never do me any riding these days anyway."

"Well, Duke will be with you tonight," Clint said. "I trust you to treat him right."

"You know it," Duffy confirmed. "But I'm afraid I've not got enough room for your wagon. You might put it 'round back. Me quarters are right about there. I be a light sleeper and if'n anybody gets a mind to mess with your possibles, I'll hear 'em sure. Won't bother me none to use me shotgun if'n I have to."

"I believe you," the Gunsmith said. "How much do I owe you?"

"Say a dollar even."

"I'll give you three dollars," Clint declared. "Take real good care of everything. Especially Duke."

"Yes sir," Duffy agreed. "Be me pleasure. Where will you be in case anything should happen and I need to get in touch with you?"

"I'll be at the Widow Malloy's place," the Gunsmith said. "Understand she's got rooms for rent."

"Reckon so." Duffy nodded. "You were talkin' to Corrigan and his chums, weren't you?"

"Yeah," Clint admitted. "Anything wrong with that?"

"Just be careful 'round those three," the hostler warned. "They can be a might wild. Know what I mean?"

DYNAMITE JUSTICE 65

"I just had a drink with them, friend."

"Only a bit of advice, mate," Duffy told him.

"Believe me," the Gunsmith assured him, "I'll remember what you've said."

After Clint was certain his wagon and horses would be taken care of, he walked to the widow's house. The Gunsmith mounted the steps and rapped on the door.

He expected a gray-haired little Irish lady to reply to the knock. Instead, the door opened to a tall, sleek redhead. She wore a blue gingham dress which failed to conceal the shapely curves of her firm young body. Her bow-shaped mouth pursed gently as she prepared to ask a question.

"Evening, ma'am," Clint began first. "I'm looking for a room for the night and I was told you have one available."

"That's right, mister," she replied. "I'm Kate Malloy. Would you care to come in and see the room?"

"Uh, yeah." The Gunsmith nodded.

He entered a small living room. It was clean and neat with simple stuffed furniture and a well-swept floor. Clint politely removed his hat and nodded his approval.

"Fine home, ma'am," the Gunsmith told her.

"Just call me Kate, Mr. . . . ?"

"Clint will do fine," he replied.

"You say you'll just be needin' the room for the night, Clint?"

"Yeah," the Gunsmith answered. "I'm moving on tomorrow."

"You just arrived this afternoon." She frowned. "But I know you got a pretty unpleasant welcome. I can't blame you for leavin' so soon."

"You know about that reception I got, eh?"

"Dublin is a tiny little town, Clint," Kate replied. "I saw you from me window this afternoon. Not likely I'd fail to recognize such a handsome stranger when he appears on my doorstep."

Clint smiled. "Thank you, Kate. Praise from a pretty lady always brightens my day."

"The feelin' be mutual, Clint." Kate grinned. "Follow me and I'll show you where you'll be sleepin' tonight."

She led the Gunsmith to the threshold of another room. Kate entered first, moving easily through the familiar darkness. She struck a match and lit a kerosene lamp on a table in the center of the room.

Yellow light bathed a brass-framed bed. Clint noticed two pillows lined with lace at the headboard. He smelled the intriguing scent of jasmine perfume. The aroma drew his attention to a vanity dresser across the room.

"Isn't this your bedroom, ma'am?" Clint asked awkwardly.

"Aye," she admitted. "Now will you be so kind as to remove your clothin' and get in the bed?"

"Well . . ." the Gunsmith didn't know how to answer such a question.

Words seemed inappropriate, so he simply began to strip. Clint naturally removed his gunbelt first and hung it on the bedpost. Kate watched him shed the rest of his clothes, then blew out the lamp flame.

"You really be a handsome man, Clint," Kate declared.

He heard the rustle of cloth as the woman disrobed. Clint saw the shapely outline of Kate's beautiful body despite the darkness. He waited until she finished before he took her in his arms.

They embraced gently until their lips met. Then fiery passion exploded within them both. Clint thrust his tongue deep inside her mouth as Kate's hands stroked his naked shoulders and chest. Fingernails raked the dark mat of hair from the center of his torso to his belly.

Clint felt Kate touch his penis. She gingerly stroked it until the fleshy member was hard and erect. He fondled her breasts and lowered his lips to the rigid nipples. Slowly, he kissed and sucked as the woman moaned in delight.

"Sure'n you've got the equipment," Kate whispered. "Now let's see how you be usin' it."

The couple moved to the bed. They practically tumbled across the mattress, unwilling to break their embrace. Clint's skillful hands traveled along Kate's soft warm flesh, caressing her into a frenzy of desire.

"Oh, Clint!" she groaned. "Don't muck about. Can't you tell I be ready, man?"

She guided him as his cock slid into her moist love chamber. He sighed with pleasure and began grinding his hips to work himself deeper. Kate gasped and dug her nails into the Gunsmith's arms. He slowly began to rock to and fro, moving in steady, smooth strokes.

Kate moaned and trembled as she neared the brink. Clint drove himself faster. Kate wrapped her long legs around his hips and pulled him closer. Kate's body bucked like a wild horse as they both climaxed.

"Lord, that was good," Kate whispered breathlessly.

"Can't argue with that," Clint admitted, gently stroking the woman's hair.

"I thought not," she laughed. "Though you probably think me quite a tart now."

"Don't be silly," he said. "No reason why a

woman shouldn't enjoy love-making as much as a man does."

"No matter," Kate sighed. "You'll be gone in the morning. Might tell your tale to the blokes you meet on the range, but you won't be spreadin' more rumors 'bout me around Dublin than already be floatin' 'bout."

"I'm not much for talking about women I've known," Clint assured her.

"Well, me husband Daniel and me didn't get along too well," Kate remarked. "But when you be married, you just have to grit your teeth and bear it. Sounds awful to admit this, but it was a bloody relief when I heard Huntington-Smythe had killed Daniel."

"I didn't know anyone had actually been killed in this feud between you folks and that man," Clint said with surprise.

"Folks in town don't talk 'bout it much," Kate replied. "You see, Huntington-Smythe claimed a couple of his men had been killed in a mine explosion. The Limey called it sabotage and, natural enough, he blamed us and told us to stay clear of his property."

"What's that have to do with Daniel's death?" Clint asked.

"Well, Daniel and a couple of his mates got a bit drunk and decided to pay Huntington-Smythe a visit. Had a practical joke in mind. Thought it would be funny to set off some bleedin' firecrackers to scare the Brit's hired blackguards. Must have worked a bit too well."

"Huntington-Smythe's men killed them?"

"Only Daniel." Kate sighed. "Other two got away without a scratch."

"I'm sorry about your husband," Clint said. "But

that was an awful stupid stunt those fellas pulled."

"No one will be arguing 'bout that," Kate admitted. "That's why nobody in town likes to talk 'bout it. Daniel and his chums went lookin' for trouble and they damn well found it. Admittin' that sort of interferes with our Irish-bred hatred of the British."

"Are you sure they went up there with just some firecrackers for a joke?" the Gunsmith asked. "And they didn't take some dynamite for a more sinister purpose?"

"Daniel wasn't a killer," she told him. "Oh, he was a minor sort of bastard. Used to drink too much and slapped me around a bit. That sort of thing. Still, he didn't have the stomach for anything as ambitious as sabotage or murder."

"Well, I'm going to see Huntington-Smythe in the morning," Clint remarked. "I'll try to talk to him about this feud. See if I can smooth things out a little."

"Blessed are the peacemakers, eh?"

"That's the reason I carry one on my hip." The Gunsmith grinned.

"That's the only type of peace the British understand," Kate stated. "Huntington-Smythe won't listen to reason."

"Can't hurt to try."

"Well, that's what you plan for tomorrow." Kate smiled. "What 'bout tonight?"

"Figured we can handle that together," Clint replied as he kissed her neck.

TWELVE

"This is getting goddamn monotonous," the Gunsmith muttered.

Once again Clint found himself facing half a dozen armed men with guns aimed at him. This time the reception committee consisted of men dressed in stetsons and denim, but they looked just as surly as the group that had confronted Clint when he rode into Dublin the day before.

"This is private property, feller," a raw-boned cowboy with a walrus mustache declared gruffly as he canted a Winchester across his shoulder.

"I know," Clint replied mildly, holding his hands at shoulder level. "That's why I'm here."

"Do tell," the cowhand mused. "Well, Mr. Huntington-Smythe ain't expectin' visitors. Especially somebody sent by those Irish jaspers."

"You guys must watch Dublin pretty close," the Gunsmith commented.

"Seems like a good idea since them Micks have been tryin' to blow up our mine," another cowboy told him.

"None of you look like coal miners to me," Clint remarked.

"Might say we're here to keep the peace," the man

who seemed to be in charge of the group stated. "If that means somebody has to *rest* in peace, so be it."

"You sound like a fella who makes his living with a gun," Clint observed. "Act like it too. You keep your gun ready, but you don't point it until you're ready to use it. Not like these nervous nellies with you."

Several of the cowboys scowled at Clint's remark.

"Noticed some things about you too, mister," the guy told Clint. "Wear your six-shooter low like a gunfighter. Mighty fine black Arabian you're ridin' too."

"Left my wagon back in Dublin."

"Do tell." The man smiled. "Then you must be the Gunsmith, right?"

An awestruck cowhand gasped.

"Rather be called Clint Adams," the Gunsmith stated. "What's your name, friend?"

"Name's Hacker," the head gunman declared. "John Hacker."

Clint nodded. "Heard of you. Used to be a deputy sheriff over in Wellsville a couple years ago."

Hacker grinned. "Didn't know I was famous."

"Maybe you'll be lucky and it won't spread," the Gunsmith told him. "Fame isn't all it's cracked up to be."

"Jesus, John," one of the gunmen growled. "Them Irish done hired Adams to be their gunfighter—"

"Then why'd he just ride up here right out in the open like this, Bob?" Hacker demanded. "Lower your hands, Clint, and tell us what this is all about."

"Sure," the Gunsmith agreed. "You guys have been posting drygulchers on the trail, right?"

"They're supposed to be sentries, not drygulchers." Hacker frowned. "Aw, shit. Don't tell me those idiots tried to ambush your wagon yesterday?''

"Okay"—Clint shrugged—"I won't tell you—but that's what happened."

Hacker sighed. "We wondered what happened to Pierce and Thomlen."

"They're still back there in the ravine," Clint replied. "I don't think they'll be going anywhere for a while. Now, I figure I'd better explain this to Huntington-Smythe before he declares war on Dublin for something the Irish didn't even do."

"Yeah," Hacker agreed. "Reckon you got a point, Clint."

Hacker walked to a number of horses tied to a nearby hitching rail, unfastened the reins of a Morgan stallion and mounted up. He turned to one of the men.

"Stan, you're in charge of the guard," he instructed.

"Right, Johnny," a stocky man with a ten-gallon hat replied with a nod.

"Clint," Hacker said, "you follow me. We're gonna see the boss."

The Gunsmith urged Duke forward till he was riding alongside the group commander. Clint glanced at the surrounding meadows where a couple dozen white-faced Herefords grazed on the tall grass.

"How big is Huntington-Smythe's spread?" the Gunsmith asked.

"The ranch isn't much," Hacker replied. "Just a thousand acres or so. Of course, the coal mines take up a lot more territory."

"Where are they?" Clint asked.

"About two miles or so over yonder," the enforcer said, pointing to some hills to the west.

Clint couldn't see the entrance to any of the mines,

but he did spot several groups of men at the base of the hills. The sound of an ore car clattering along iron rails reached the Gunsmith. An involuntary shudder rode up his spine. Clint had good reason to remember that sound.

He had nearly been killed by such a car in a Nevada silver mine several years before.*

"How long have you been working for Huntington-Smythe?" Clint asked.

"About a month," Hacker replied. "The major hired most of us about then after the trouble with the Irish started."

"They say they didn't start it," the Gunsmith remarked.

"Reckon they'd admit it if they had?" Hacker shrugged. "Look, Clint. I don't know what the beef is about. I'm not sure who started what first. I was a sergeant in the Confederate Army during the War Between the States and I didn't know what the hell we were fighting for, or who started that mess either. I'm just hired to protect the major's property."

"Those two guys who tried to blast me on the trail weren't defending this place," the Gunsmith commented.

"They made a mistake," Hacker stated. "We're getting close to the major's house. You can talk to him about it."

"Why do you call Huntington-Smythe 'the major'?" Clint asked.

"He was formerly a major in the British Army," Hacker explained. "Corps of engineers or something like that. Sort of a stuffed shirt at times, but he's okay, I reckon."

---

* *The Gunsmith #17: Silver War*

They approached a trio of buildings among the shade of a cluster of trees. A number of horses were corralled behind a large barn. Clint guessed a long rectangular structure was probably a bunkhouse—or a barracks. However, the two men headed straight for a house which resembled an oversized cottage.

Huntington-Smythe's home was made of brown stone and mortar. Ivy vines clung to the framework of the porch. *Quaint,* a word which seldom entered the Gunsmith's thoughts, was how he would have had to describe it.

Clint and Hacker dismounted and hitched their horses to a rail in front of the house and then stepped onto the porch. Hacker prepared to knock, but the door opened before his knuckles could strike it.

The Gunsmith's eyes widened with surprise and interest when he saw a very pretty young girl before him. She appeared to be in her late teens or early twenties. The girl's dark brown hair was fashioned in an inappropriate bun to accommodate an ecru net and a white lace cap. A white serving apron was tied around her waist.

"I heard you ride up," the girl explained. "Is something wrong, Mr. Hacker?"

"Gotta talk to the major, Christine," Hacker told her. "Could you let him know I've got a visitor for him? Explain to him that a couple of our boys made a mighty big mistake that got 'em both killed."

"Oh, dear," Christine gasped. Her big soft brown eyes met Clint's gaze. "And what name shall I give the major?"

"Clint Adams," the Gunsmith replied.

Christine hurried away. Clint watched the sway of her rump as she trotted across the carpeted floor of a parlor.

"Pretty girl," the Gunsmith remarked. "She sounds like an American. She's not the major's daughter, is she?"

"Christine is Huntington-Smythe's maid," Hacker replied. "And his mistress."

"Oh," Clint sighed. "Well, I admire his taste."

A minute later, Christine returned. "The major will see you now. He's waiting in his office. Will you please follow me?"

"A pleasure," Clint whispered, his eyes once again trained on Christine's backside.

THIRTEEN

Major Huntington-Smythe wore a monocle. Clint Adams had never seen a man with a monocle up close before. The single-lens eyepiece dominated the Gunsmith's attention as he examined the Briton's face.

Actually, Huntington-Smythe's features were rather bland and nondescript. Perhaps that was why he wore the monocle. Yet the man's rigid posture and dignity labeled him as more than an average man.

The major sat behind a huge oakwood desk. A fancy white helmet and an officer's saber hung from a wall rack. There were several bookshelves filled with leather-bound volumes. A brass replica of an artillery cannon sat in one corner.

"I wondered what happened to Pierce and Thomlen," Huntington-Smythe declared, after listening to Clint's story.

"I'm surprised your men didn't find their graves," the Gunsmith remarked. "I covered them with rocks to keep the scavengers off the bodies. Your boys ought to find them easily enough."

"How very decent of you, Mr. Adams," the major replied with a cultured Cambridge accent. "Well, I'm very sorry about this. Of course, the men had orders to scare off any of the Irish scum who might be bringing in supplies. They weren't supposed to harass passersby."

"Harass, hell," Clint said sharply. "Those guys tried to kill me, Major."

"Hacker?" Huntington-Smythe turned to his foreman. "What do you think?"

"I didn't know Pierce or Thomlen well enough to figure how reliable they would be." The former lawman shrugged. "But I've got some doubts about several of these young jaspers you hired. Bob Flick and Jeb Sommers are two fellers I don't reckon we'd better put on duty by the ravine."

"So you're inclined to believe Mr. Adams's story?"

"Yes sir." Hacker nodded. "He's got a rep as being a man of his word and I don't reckon he would have killed those two idiots unless they provoked him, sir."

"Very well," the major sighed. "I'm sorry, Mr. Adams."

"Me too," Clint assured him.

"But circumstances merit more than an apology," Huntington-Smythe added. "If there is any way I can repay you for the problems caused by this unfortunate incident, please tell me."

"Well, I spent the night in Dublin," Clint began.

"How much did you spend on room and board?" the Briton inquired. "I'll be happy to pay for your expenses—"

"That's not necessary, Major," the Gunsmith told him. "The point is, I heard a lot about this feud between you and those Irish folks. I've listened to their side and now I'd like to hear yours."

"The Irish started the feud, Mr. Adams," Huntington-Smythe declared. "Not I."

"They see it differently," Clint said.

"I'm sure they told you they were innocent victims." The Briton sighed. "The Irish have a habit of inciting violence. They tend to pick fights they can't win, and then complain about the outcome when they lose. Naturally, they have to accuse the victor of being the aggressor. It's typical of their breed, Mr. Adams."

Clint shrugged. "I heard similar stories about how you're being typically British. So far, all I know for sure is you and the people of Dublin both bear a pretty big grudge."

"Prejudice isn't always wrong," Huntington-Smythe replied. "Often there's a solid reason for it."

"You're obviously an intelligent man, Major," the Gunsmith began. "You should know that you never judge a man by his reputation—or some silly idea other people have about him."

"I've had some bad experiences with the Irish," Huntington-Smythe said sternly.

"Sounds like they've had some bad experiences with the British, too," Clint went on. "None of which has much to do with your group or the town of Dublin. At least it shouldn't. Hell, I was kicked by a horse more than once, but I don't hate all four-legged animals because that happened."

"You're a remarkably civilized man for an American, Mr. Adams." The Briton smiled.

"You'd be surprised, Major." Clint grinned. "Some of us Americans can read and write."

"I didn't mean that as an insult," Huntington-Smythe assured him. "As you know, I've got a coal mining operation here. I've been setting this business up for almost two years. I've invested a great deal of time, money and effort into this project. Finally, it's beginning to make a profit."

"Nothing wrong with making a profit," Clint said. "I try to do that myself. That's not the problem, is it?"

"Bloody well is when Irish hoodlums sabotage one of my mines," the Briton replied angrily. "They dynamited a shaft and killed three of my men."

"Dynamite can be pretty unstable at times," Clint remarked. "I'm no explosives expert, but I know dynamite can get mighty touchy when it gets old or it hasn't been stored properly."

"I happen to be familiar with explosives, Mr. Adams," Huntington-Smythe said stiffly. "I was formerly a military engineer. I know how to use dynamite."

"The major personally sees to the explosives used here," Hacker told Clint. "I understand about twenty pounds of dynamite froze last winter and he refused to let it be used."

"Frozen dynamite is stable enough," the Briton explained. "But it's too dangerous when it begins to thaw. It becomes highly unpredictable. I couldn't let my men try to use it."

"The miners told me that the major personally disposed of the dynamite," Hacker added, his tone revealing respect for his employer. "Didn't let anybody go with him when he hauled it to a safe place and detonated it."

"I'm not denying the major's expertise," Clint assured them. "But one of the miners could have made a mistake even if the dynamite was in good condition."

"And this *accident* just happened to occur after the Irish set up Dublin?" Huntington-Smythe remarked dryly. "Odd coincidence, isn't it?"

"But it could have been just that," Clint said.

"After it happened I warned the Irish to stay away

from my property," the Briton continued. "But some of them still insisted on sneaking in here."

"I was told that was a practical joke," Clint told him. "Most of the townsfolk in Dublin think it was pretty stupid of the fellas who did it."

"A practical joke?" Huntington-Smythe scoffed. "They crept onto my property and tried to shoot my men. You call that a practical joke?"

"I heard those guys just set off some firecrackers to scare your men," the Gunsmith stated.

"That's a friggin' lie," Hacker snapped. "I was on duty that night. The Irish set off some firecrackers, that's true. But they also fired pistols at us. We shot back at 'em and killed one of the bastards."

"Are you sure they shot at you?" Clint asked.

"Jesus, Clint," Hacker growled. "I've been shot at before. You know what that's like. Figure you could mistake some firecrackers for a pistol shot?"

"Okay." The Gunsmith nodded. "Maybe there's more involved than I know about. Could be some hotheads among the Irish—"

"Hotheads?" Huntington-Smythe's monocle fell when he raised his eyebrow. "Or Fenians?"

"What are Fenians?" Clint asked.

"They call themselves guerrilla fighters," the major explained. "In other words, they specialize in shooting British soldiers in the back. One of their leaders is a butcher named Mackey Lomasey who operates in the Cork area of Ireland. Calls himself the 'Little Captain.' Surprised you never heard of the murdering little runt since he learned his sneaky killing tactics as an officer in the Union Army during the War Between the States, here in America."

"Never heard of Fenians in this country," Hacker

commented. "But I've heard plenty about another Irish outlaw group."

"The Molly Maguires," Clint said before Hacker got a chance to mention the secret society.

"I see you're not totally ignorant of Irish violence," Huntington-Smythe remarked.

"All kinds of folks commit violence," the Gunsmith said. "There's no evidence to suggest the people in Dublin are Molly Maguires."

"After what's happened to us," the Briton said, replacing his monocle, "we don't need any more proof."

"I do," Clint Adams declared. "And maybe I know how to find some answers, one way or the other."

FOURTEEN

The Gunsmith returned to Dublin later that afternoon and headed straight for Sean O'Hara's home. Clint dismounted. There wasn't a hitching rail in front of the mayor's house, but Duke was too well-trained to wander off.

The only reason Clint ever bothered to tie the gelding to a rail was to discourage horse thieves. If anybody figured Duke was an invitation to steal an unhitched horse, the would-be thief would soon find out differently. Duke would probably stomp the fellow to death before Clint could get a chance to shoot the bastard.

Maureen O'Hara answered the door. She smiled and fluffed her drab gray hair when she saw who her visitor was. Clint politely tipped his stetson and asked if her husband was home.

"Aye," she replied, pursing her wide, full lips. "Please come in, Mr. Adams."

Clint entered, but he didn't see Sean O'Hara. Maureen strolled over to the table and slid out one of the chairs.

"Please have a seat, Mr. Adams," she invited, "and I'll fetch you some whiskey while you wait."

"Wait?" Clint frowned. "You said your husband was here, Mrs. O'Hara?"

"Sure'n he is," Maureen replied, placing both hands on her wide hips. "But he's takin' a nap. I'll wake him just as soon as I make you comfortable."

"I appreciate your hospitality," Clint assured her as he lowered himself into the chair. "But I don't care for any whiskey. A little early in the day for me."

"Wish Sean felt that way." Maureen sighed. "Pity that a man can take to liquor so. He's sleepin' off a drunk right now."

"Some fellas can sure make a habit of it," the Gunsmith agreed.

He recalled how his best friend, James Hickok, had become addicted to the bottle. Following the murder of Wild Bill, Clint had also taken to strong drink for a while, but he managed to crawl out of the alcoholic trap before it could destroy him.*

"Look," Clint went on, "I wanted to talk to Sean about Corrigan and his two buddies Durkan and O'Quinn."

"What about them?" Maureen frowned.

"I think they might be Molly Maguires."

"That's a rash statement," she told him. "Sure'n they were coal miners back in Pennsylvania, but that's no reason to think they're Mollies."

"You figure they are too, don't you?" Clint asked, staring into her eyes to watch for a reaction.

"I didn't say that," Maureen looked away. "But I know they be troublemakers when they put their minds to it . . . which is *too* often, if'n you be askin' me."

"Like that incident when Daniel Malloy was killed?" the Gunsmith asked.

"I'm surprised you know about that," Maureen

* *The Gunsmith #14: Dead Man's Hand*

said. "Not the sort of thing most of us be talkin' 'bout."

"Two of Malloy's mates went with him to harass Huntington-Smythe's men," Clint said. "I figure those fellas were Durkan and O'Quinn. Right?"

"Aye," Maureen confessed. "How did you guess?"

"I doubt that you folks came out here with a supply of firecrackers," Clint answered. "Since the three guys who played that so-called joke took firecrackers with them, somebody must have made them for the occasion. Who would that person be? Durkan is an explosives expert. Figures that he'd know how to whip up some firecrackers. He's good pals with Corrigan and O'Quinn, so it makes sense that one of them was the third man involved that night. Corrigan is too smart to actually participate in something like that. So that leaves O'Quinn."

"That just proves that drunken Irishmen can be foolish," Maureen said. "It doesn't mean the Mollies are involved."

"No," Clint admitted as he rose from his chair. "But I think I know who to talk to now."

"Where be you off to, Clint Adams?" Maureen demanded, watching him head for the door.

"To see how somebody reacts to a few blunt questions," the Gunsmith replied simply.

FIFTEEN

Old Duffy, the hostler, gazed up when Clint Adams entered the Glenmalure Tavern. Duffy and another elderly man were seated at a table sharing a pitcher of beer and playing checkers. They were the only customers. Jack Corrigan stood behind the bar rinsing out mugs and glasses. He paused to wave at the Gunsmith.

"Welcome back, mate," Corrigan greeted cheerfully. "Came to have one last glass of Irish pleasure before you be leavin' Dublin for good, eh?"

"I want to talk to you, Jack," Clint replied. He turned to Duffy. "Maybe you and your friend could continue your game outside. I'd best talk to Jack alone. Okay?"

"Bloody well ain't okay with me," Duffy's companion replied gruffly. "You got no right to tell us to leave . . ."

"Clint just made a suggestion," Duffy said quickly. "And I think it be wise if'n we follow his advice, Art."

The elderly pair shuffled out the door. Corrigan gazed at the Gunsmith's right hand which hovered close to the grips of the .45 Colt holstered on his hip. The Irishman placed his hands palms down on the counter.

"You seem a mite disturbed, Clint," he remarked. "What bothers you, man?"

"I understand your friends O'Quinn and Durkan paid a visit to Huntington-Smythe's property a while back," the Gunsmith began. "A fella named Malloy was killed because of that incident."

"Been pokin' around quite a bit, now haven't you?" Corrigan mused. "I supposed Malloy's widow told you 'bout this?"

"I got information from a couple sources and crosschecked it for accuracy," Clint replied as he approched the bar.

Corrigan laughed. "You're a regular detective. If you don't mind workin' for a real son of a bitch, you might think 'bout joinin' Alan Pinkerton's group."

"I'll work for myself," Clint said. "That way I don't have anybody to blame my mistakes on. Now tell me about that night."

"All right." The Irishman sighed. "So O'Quinn and Durkan joined Malloy for that stupid firecracker joke."

"It wasn't a joke," the Gunsmith said. "Durkan and O'Quinn convinced Malloy to go with them. He was a drunk and a bully by nature so they probably just had to get him liquored up enough to agree to the plan. Then they went up to Huntington-Smythe's place and took a couple shots at his men."

"Who told you that?" Corrigan asked. "I suppose it must have been the Limey."

"Huntington-Smythe's foreman agrees that your friends fired pistols that night."

"And you believe him?" Corrigan shook his head. "You'd rather take the word of a rich Englishman and his lacky than believe the hard-workin' Irish here in Dublin, eh?"

"The people in Dublin are okay," Clint told him. "Except they're full of hatred for the English. Of course, Huntington-Smythe is just as prejudiced against the Irish. Now, who would have something to gain by exploiting the hate of both the Irish and the Briton?"

"I imagine you think that person would be me," Corrigan remarked.

The Gunsmith nodded. "You, Durkan and O'Quinn. I doubt that there are any more Molly Maguires in town."

"There are other former coal miners from Pennsylvania here," Corrigan replied. "Why don't you suspect them too?"

"They don't take orders from you, Jack," Clint said. "They don't lick your boots and praise your genius like O'Quinn and Durkan. You three are Molly Maguires and you, Jack Corrigan, are the leader of the pack."

"That's a wild accusation, Clint," Corrigan told him. "You've got no proof. Do you?"

"The explosion in the mine," Clint said. "Durkan could manage that easily enough."

"The Englishman's powderman was careless. It was an accident and he blamed us for it."

"And then Durkan and O'Quinn just happen to be part of that firecracker stunt," the Gunsmith continued. "That must have been your idea. You're a clever fella, Jack. You came up with a good plan, even if it didn't quite work as well as you'd hoped."

"Really?" The Irishman laughed. "And what was me plan, Clint?"

"You needed a martyr," Clint began. "Nothing helps a righteous cause more than a dead martyr slain by the enemy. So you planned to get Malloy killed.

O'Quinn and Durkan fired their guns at Huntington-Smythe's men and let Malloy catch a bullet or two. Then they probably used the firecrackers as a distraction to help them escape."

Corrigan chuckled. "Doesn't sound like such a bad scheme at that."

"Would have worked better if Malloy hadn't told his wife where he was going, and why," Clint said. "Everybody in Dublin figured it was just a dumb practical joke that got out of hand. You didn't get the desired effect because nobody shed any tears over Malloy, but it was still successful because it served to cause more tension on both sides of the feud. The Briton decided to cut off supplies to try to starve the people of Dublin into leaving and the townsfolk have become more fearful and suspicious."

"And why would I want to be doin' all this mischief, Clint?" Corrigan asked, folding his arms on his chest.

"Two reasons," the Gunsmith began. "First, you figure you can take over this town. O'Hara isn't strong enough to lead these people under stress. He's too fond of the bottle. You're just waiting to take his place."

"Aye." Corrigan rolled his eyes at the ceiling. "And what poor lad of the sod from Cork wouldn't be dyin' to inherit a miserable little hamlet like Dublin to rule over like a bloody lord? Be serious, mate."

"This town would be worth plenty if you could also seize control of the mines," Clint added. "Drive out Huntington-Smythe and you can just move in and take charge. Dublin becomes your very own mining town. Don't tell me you can't see a potential for profit in that."

"Profit and power," Corrigan admitted. "I lived under the yoke of British rulers long enough to see how it works."

"And to acquire a desire to do likewise yourself," the Gunsmith commented.

"You forget," Corrigan began, "I was one of the oppressed, not an oppressor."

"Suffering doesn't always build character," Clint declared. "As often as not it makes a man bitter, selfish and cruel. You saw a chance to seize power and you're going after it by using the only methods you know—the ones you learned from the Molly Maguires."

"Bullshit," Corrigan scoffed. "Your theory only proves you've got a wild imagination, Clint. Why are you telling me this? If you can prove any of these claims you ought to go to see Mayor O'Hara, or the federal marshals, or whatever." Corrigan smiled at the Gunsmith. "Ah, Clint," he sighed. "You came here to tell me all this wild nonsense in the hopes I'd be obligin' and break down for you. Expected me to confess to all me sins. Call a ruddy town meetin' for ol' Jack to make his confession. Send for a hangman and a priest with a strong stomach. Jack Corrigan is turnin' himself in. Doesn't that all seem a bit silly now, Clint?"

"We'll see, Jack," the Gunsmith replied as he turned to leave.

"Clint," the Irishman called out. "I've taken a likin' to you, lad. You're a bold man, but you've decided to mix into somethin' that is really not your concern. Leave it be, Clint. Ride out of Dublin and forget you were ever here, man."

"And if I don't?" Clint asked, glancing over his shoulder at the Irishman.

"Well"—Corrigan shrugged—"then do stop again and have a drink next time. The Glenmalure needs payin' customers, don't you know."

SIXTEEN

As the Gunsmith emerged from the tavern he caught a glimpse of a figure which darted behind the corner of the Glenmalure. Clint's hand fell to his six-gun in case someone was waiting to ambush him. He wasn't certain, but the size of the figure suggested it may have been Durkan.

He walked forward slowly, glancing about for any telltale signs of attackers. Durkan may have listened at the door of the Glenmalure and heard Clint's conversation with Corrigan. Not too important as Corrigan would probably tell his comrades about Clint's visit anyway.

Unless Durkan, O'Quinn or both men decided to take some kind of action on their own before consulting with Corrigan.

The Gunsmith would have almost welcomed that. He had hoped Durkan or O'Quinn would be tending bar when he entered the Glenmalure. He'd planned to spring his theory on one of Corrigan's underlings because he figured they'd be more apt to react rashly to such a confrontation.

Perhaps they would have, but Jack Corrigan himself had kept his head with admirable calm. Nonetheless, Clint was certain his theory was correct. The trio were

Molly Maguires and they were trying to pit both sides of the feud against each other.

But Corrigan did have a point. Dublin and Huntington-Smythe were not the Gunsmith's problem. Why should he get caught in the middle of their war? Both sides were mule-headed and blinded by prejudice. Why should Clint stick his neck out for any of them?

Curiosity, the Gunsmith realized. He could never resist a mystery or a chance for adventure. More than once he'd gotten himself in trouble because he was curious or craved excitement.

Not this time, the Gunsmith decided.

He headed for the livery stable. Duffy and his friend Art were seated on kegs, once again playing checkers. The hostler immediately rose from his seat when he saw the Gunsmith. Art muttered a sour remark under his breath.

"Sorry to interrupt you guys again," Clint said. "But I'd like to get my wagon ready to leave."

"Oh," the hostler frowned. "Thought you'd be stayin' for a while."

"I figure I've done enough for a bunch of folks who seem determined to fight anyway. I plan to be on my way and leave this town to work out its own problems."

"Can't say as I can blame you for that," the old man sighed. "Guess your conversation with Jack Corrigan didn't turn out too well."

"He didn't say anything to change my mind," Clint replied. "But he didn't say anything to help me either. By the way, does *Glenmalure* mean anything special or did Corrigan just name the tavern after his favorite brand of whiskey?"

"Glenmalure was the site of a great victory in Ireland," Duffy explained. "Happened sometime in the fourteenth century, as I recall. Fiach MacHugh O'Byrne defeated the Brits at Glenmalure. O'Byrne was sort of the first Irish guerrilla warfare hero and the battle at Glenmalure showed how well such tactics can work."

"Figures Corrigan would name his saloon something corny like that," the Gunsmith muttered.

Duffy shrugged. "Not so corny for a fella who might be a Molly Maguire."

The Gunsmith glared at him. "You already knew that Corrigan was a Molly Maguire?"

"Can't say as I knew it exactly," the old man replied. "But I figure everybody in town always assumed Jack and his mates O'Quinn and Durkan are all Molly Maguires. Things are getting a bit rough for the Mollies back in Pennsylvania. Hell, the police know damn good and well John Kehoe is more or less the leader. They just haven't been able to prove it yet."

"You mean everybody suspects Corrigan and his pals are Mollies who fled West to escape the gallows," Clint began, "but nobody in town is willing to accept the possibility he started this trouble with Huntington-Smythe?"

"You don't understand these folks, Clint." Duffy smiled. "They've been hatin' the British so long, they can't help being pissed at the Limey. Besides, when our men went to the mines lookin' for jobs, the Brit called 'em Irish filth and refused to hire 'em. When that explosion occurred in his mine, he blamed all of us for it. So we all took offense and blamed him back. What about his tryin' to starve us out by blockin' all supplies into Dublin? Course we don't like Huntington-Smythe and we resent him more than we do Jack Corrigan."

"That's dumb," Clint growled. "You folks might wind up in a full scale war with Huntington-Smythe. And I'll tell you something—if that happens, Dublin will lose."

"We Irish ain't so easily defeated, laddie," Art snapped angrily.

"I've been up to Huntington-Smythe's spread," the Gunsmith stated. "He's got at least half a dozen gunhawks on his payroll. At least one of those fellas is a pro. That's not including any of the miners working for him who might join the gunmen if they decide to hit Dublin. They'll tear you people up if it comes to that."

"I doubt that'll happen," Duffy said. "Things are a bit tense, but we won't start killin' each other—"

"For God's sake," Clint groaned. "The killing has already started . . ."

"Excuse me," a feminine voice called softly. "But would you be Clint Adams?"

The Gunsmith turned to see an attractive young blond girl with big blue eyes and a bigger chest. Her breasts strained the fabric of her cotton dress. When she stepped forward, Clint half expected her to fall into his arms. He wouldn't have objected if that had happened, but the girl managed to defy gravity as she walked quickly toward him.

"Mr. Adams?" she repeated.

"Please call me Clint," he replied with a smile.

"I must talk to you, Clint," the girl said urgently. "Could you please come with me?"

"Sure," the Gunsmith agreed.

"Wait a minute, Clint . . ." Duffy began.

"I'll be back after a bit," the Gunsmith told him.

"Don't harness the team to my wagon. I'll help you with that. Okay?"

"But Clint . . ." Duffy insisted.

However, the Gunsmith's attention was centered on the blonde so he failed to notice the urgency in the hostler's voice. Clint followed the girl to a small house near the livery.

"Now what's this about, Miss—?"

"O'Toole," she replied. "Bridgett O'Toole. I want to talk to you 'bout the Molly Maguires."

"Lady, you sure know how to get my attention," Clint told her. "I'm listening."

The couple approached the entrance of the house. Bridgett opened the door and led Clint inside. The room was small, and had dust-covered furniture and a pile of dirty clothes in one corner. The girl was pretty, but she sure had a lot to learn about keeping house.

Then Clint noticed a man's denim work shirt draped over the back of a chair. He also detected the stench of stale, used cigars. Either Bridgett O'Toole had some very masculine tastes, or a husband.

"Maybe this isn't a good place to talk," Clint suggested. A sixth sense alerted him to the possibility that he'd just been led into a trap.

Bridgett's sudden scream confirmed this. The Gunsmith whirled, reaching for his Colt instinctively. The girl had deliberately ripped open the front of her dress as she shrieked for help. Clint didn't enjoy the generous display of cleavage. He was too busy trying to decide what the hell he should do.

The door burst open. Mike O'Quinn's enormous form stormed through the entrance with a Winchester carbine in his fists and a vicious smile on his wide face.

SEVENTEEN

O'Quinn spent a fraction of a second training his weapon on the Gunsmith. That was all the time Clint needed to draw his Colt revolver. O'Quinn gasped when he found himself staring into the muzzle of Clint's pistol even as he aimed the Winchester at the Gunsmith.

"You can either put down that gun and we'll talk," Clint declared. "Or pull the trigger and we'll die together."

O'Quinn glared at the Gunsmith. Clint's steady gaze and poker face warned him that the Gunsmith meant what he said. The Irishman's face tensed. He ground his teeth together in frustration. Slowly, he began to lower the Winchester.

Without warning, Bridgett O'Toole seized Clint's wrist. She shoved forcibly and pushed the modified Colt toward the floor.

O'Quinn didn't fire his Winchester, afraid he might hit the girl. Instead, the big Irishman stormed forward and swung the buttstock of the carbine at Clint's head.

The Gunsmith ducked under the whirling walnut and simultaneously jabbed his left fist under O'Quinn's ribs.

O'Quinn groaned.

Clint howled.

Bridgett had bitten his hand to force him to drop the Colt revolver.

The Irish brute prepared to swing the Winchester buttstock again. The Gunsmith quickly pivoted to haul Bridgett O'Toole into his opponent. Man and woman staggered backward.

Clint lunged forward and pounced into O'Quinn like a puma attacking a bull bison. Both men gripped the frame of the Winchester as they stumbled through the open doorway. They tumbled into the dust outside and continued to struggle for possession of the carbine.

The Gunsmith was only vaguely aware of the crowd which formed around the combatants. He was too busy fighting an opponent who outweighed him by at least fifty pounds—and none of it seemed to be fat. O'Quinn's size and weight were a great advantage in such a wrestling match. He soon managed to pin Clint to the ground and pressed the frame of the Winchester across the Gunsmith's throat.

"O'Quinn!" a voice shouted.

The Irish hulk ignored it and shoved the carbine harder. Clint strained to push the Winchester from his throat, but O'Quinn's weight and muscle power were too great. The carbine cut off Clint's breath and threatened to crush his windpipe. He stared up at O'Quinn's savage, grinning features as the Irishman continued to throttle him.

"Goddamn it, O'Quinn," a different voice snarled.

Suddenly, O'Quinn yelped in pain when a boot struck flesh. The terrible crushing weight vanished from Clint's throat as O'Quinn tumbled off him. Jack Corrigan towered over the Gunsmith. He folded his arms on his chest and smiled down at Clint.

"Didn't anyone ever tell you lads that only dogs fight in public?" he asked.

"Bloody damn!" O'Quinn complained. "You kicked me, Jack!"

"That's your own fault," Corrigan replied mildly. "You wouldn't listen when I yelled at you, and I had to get your attention somehow."

"I found Adams in me bleedin' house," O'Quinn declared as he climbed to his feet and thrust the Winchester at Clint. "The bastard was tryin' to rape me wife!"

"How about that, Clint?" Corrigan inquired.

"She told me her name was Bridgett O'Toole," Clint replied hoarsely, rubbing his throat as he got up. "Said she had to talk to me about—"

"And you tried to rape her, you bastard!" O'Quinn roared, putting the carbine to his shoulder.

"Quit muckin' about with that gun, O'Quinn," Sean O'Hara commanded as he strode forward with his shillelagh walking stick. "Put it down, O'Quinn."

"Keep out of this, O'Hara," the big man snapped.

"I'm still the mayor."

"I don't give a fuck if you're Saint Patrick," O'Quinn snapped. "Adams was messin' 'bout with me wife."

"Her maiden name was O'Toole, right?" O'Hara asked with a smile. "Now why would she be callin' herself by that instead of tellin' Clint she be Mrs. Bridgett O'Quinn?"

"She wouldn't have done that," O'Quinn replied. "Adams must be lyin'."

"He probably overheard somebody sayin' that Bridgett's name be O'Toole," Timothy Durkan supplied, coming to the aid of his friend. "And he didn't know that she be Mike's wife."

"Aye," Corrigan added. "Seems to me this is all just a misunderstandin'."

"A misunderstandin'?" O'Quinn stared at him in astonishment. "Adams forced hisself on Bridgett and I'm . . ."

"And who can blame him for wantin' to do that?" Corrigan grinned. "I imagine every man here has felt an urge to do the same. Maybe you should have married an ugly girl instead, O'Quinn."

A number of voices chuckled at the remark. O'Quinn's face became beet red and his fists tightened around the Winchester.

"Course, none of us would be doin' such a thing," Corrigan added quickly. "But Clint didn't know she be your wife. I'm sure he didn't hurt her or get a chance to violate poor Bridgett, so you needn't get quite so worked up 'bout this, O'Quinn."

"Clint be fixin' to leave Dublin anyway," Duffy announced. "Why don't we just let him go and forget about this?"

"After what he done?" O'Quinn bellowed. "I'm gonna kill the son of a London slut—"

"No," Corrigan said sharply. "There'll be no killin', O'Quinn."

"But, Jack . . ." O'Quinn began hopelessly.

"I told you no and that's the end of it, lad," Corrigan insisted as if chiding a child.

"No man shames me like this, Jack," O'Quinn warned. "Not even you."

"Damn it, man!" Corrigan snapped. "I not be tryin' to shame you. I'm just tryin' to keep you from murder. Killin' Clint is a wee bit extreme for what he done to Bridgett—since he didn't have time to do much."

DYNAMITE JUSTICE 103

The crowd laughed. The Gunsmith didn't. He was still trying to figure out what sort of game the Molly Maguires were playing. Whatever it was, his life was on the line.

"So," Corrigan continued, "instead of killin' the poor horny bloke, why don't you just give him a proper thrashin', O'Quinn?"

"A thrashin'?" The big man smiled happily.

"Aye," Corrigan replied. "You can manage that, can't you?"

"Be a bloody picnic," O'Quinn nodded.

"Then beat the hell out of him and we'll send him from Dublin with plenty of bruises and such to remind him not to be so forward with a lady in the future."

"Wait a minute," O'Hara began. "That ain't no fair fight. O'Quinn is almost twice as big as Clint."

Corrigan shrugged. "Nothin' we can do about that."

"Come on, Adams," O'Quinn grinned. "Let's see how good you are without your bleedin' six-gun."

"Jesus," the Gunsmith rasped as he watched the big man ball his fists and charge, an Irish freight train coming straight for him.

O'Quinn swung a wild roundhouse punch at Clint's head. The Gunsmith weaved out of the path of the fist. He rammed his right fist under O'Quinn's heart and hooked a left to the side of the larger man's jaw. O'Quinn didn't even grunt.

The big Irishman suddenly shoved his right forearm into Clint. The Gunsmith staggered backward as O'Quinn followed up with a left hook that caught Clint on the cheekbone. Clint fell heavily on his back. O'Quinn whooped in victory and swung a boot at Clint's face.

The Gunsmith's hands flashed. He caught

O'Quinn's foot before the kick could strike its intended target. O'Quinn growled like an angry bear as he hopped on one foot, trying to force the other down with all his weight behind it in a vicious stomp.

Clint lashed out a leg and thrust his boot between O'Quinn's splayed legs. The Irishman shrieked in agony when the kick smashed into his testicles. O'Quinn convulsed in pain. The Gunsmith twisted his opponent's ankle and threw O'Quinn off balance.

"Foul, Clint!" Corrigan laughed. "Didn't know you had it in you, mate!"

"Come on, Mike!" Durkan shouted. "Get up and bash that bastard!"

Clint rose first. O'Quinn dragged himself to one knee and glared up at the Gunsmith. Suddenly, he bolted forward like a striking rattler. Clint swung a right cross, but his knuckles only grazed O'Quinn's hard skull as the big man charged low.

O'Quinn wrapped his powerful arms around Clint's trunk and applied a brutal bear hug. He fastened his hands together at the small of Clint's spine and squeezed. His strong forearms constricted the Gunsmith's waist under the ribcage and pressed against the kidneys as if trying to crush them into pulp—which was exactly what O'Quinn intended to do.

Clint didn't waste time trying to pry himself from the larger man's deadly embrace. He quickly swung both arms hard and clapped his palms against the sides of O'Quinn's head. The Gunsmith then snapped his head forward and butted the front of his skull into the bridge of the Irishman's nose.

O'Quinn cried out and released his opponent. The big man staggered backward and clamped both hands to his ringing ears. Blood trickled from his nostrils.

The Gunsmith didn't give him time to recover. Clint slammed a right cross to O'Quinn's face, followed by a hard left hook. O'Quinn's eyes glazed. Clint hit him under the jaw with an uppercut. The Irishman's head bounced from the blow and Clint clipped him on the point of the chin with a left jab.

Mike O'Quinn swayed like a drunkard. Then his eyes closed and he crashed to the ground. Clint stood over his opponent until he was certain the Irishman was unconscious.

"Well, I'll be damned," Tim Durkan said in a stunned voice.

"I sure hope so," the Gunsmith muttered as he walked unsteadily from the still form of Mike O'Quinn.

"Congratulations, Clint," Corrigan declared. "Looks like you'll be leavin' here as winner."

"Then I'll be the only one," the Gunsmith replied. "The way things are going in this town, you'll all be losers before it's over."

EIGHTEEN

The Gunsmith drove his wagon out of Dublin less than an hour after the fight with Mike O'Quinn. Clint headed south, back toward the town of Holden. He hoped Huntington-Smythe's men had been told to be more careful about who they shot at. Clint didn't relish encountering another ambush at the ravine.

"You know what happened back there in Dublin, big fella?" Clint called to Duke as they approached the mountain pass.

Tied to the rear of the wagon by a guideline, Duke neighed in reply. Clint saw the horse raise and lower his head as if to nod.

"You do, huh?" the Gunsmith muttered. "Then you figured out that Durkan and O'Quinn probably overheard my conversation with Corrigan and came up with that dumb plan to use Bridgett to lure me into a trap. Maybe it wasn't all that dumb. It almost worked. She was supposed to cry rape and O'Quinn was then supposed to burst into the place and shoot me. Would have been sort of hard for me to protest my innocence after I'd been killed."

Clint glanced at the surrounding rock walls with suspicion as they traveled into the ravine.

"When the plan went sour," he continued, "Corrigan came to my rescue because he didn't want O'Quinn to choke me to death in front of the whole town. Jack's a smart hoot owl. He managed to turn his men's blunder into a moral victory for himself.''

The Gunsmith heard something move among the rocks. He reached for the Springfield carbine under his seat. A large rabbit scurried across the stony rubble at the base of a mountain and darted for a burrow. Clint sighed with relief.

"So Corrigan showed everybody how well he could take command. O'Hara couldn't stop O'Quinn from killing me, but Corrigan didn't have any trouble controlling the guy. He handled that incident like a seasoned politician and emerged as the wise warrior who refuses to shed blood unless there is no other choice.''

Duke whinnied loudly.

"Hey, just because I respect Corrigan's intelligence doesn't mean I admire the guy,'' Clint told his horse. "He's a dangerous troublemaker and he's leading the people of Dublin into a confrontation with Huntington-Smythe—one that will probably end in a hell of a bloodbath. So what am I supposed to do? Go back there and get in the middle of their feud?''

Duke neighed even louder.

"Look,'' the Gunsmith insisted, "I tried to help, didn't I? Dublin isn't my concern. Why should I always get mixed up in other people's problems? Hell, I'm getting too old to be—''

Duke suddenly bolted away from the wagon. The powerful animal violently yanked the guideline which snapped like a strand of weak twine.

"Duke!'' Clint exclaimed as he pulled the reins to bring the wagon to an abrupt halt. "What the hell is—''

Then the Gunsmith realized he had failed to pay attention to Duke's urgent call. The gelding had been trying to warn him that they were in danger.

"Oh, shit," Clint rasped as he reached for the Springfield.

A sudden movement among the rock rubble caught Clint's attention. A huge figure rose up from the stony shelter and pointed a pair of iron cylinders at the Gunsmith.

Clint wasn't in position to quick-draw his Colt and there wasn't time to use the Springfield. He threw himself from the wagon as the shotgun roared. The Gunsmith hit the ground hard, tumbling on impact to reduce the chance of injury. He rolled to the closest wagon wheel for cover and drew his modified Colt revolver.

The wheel moved forward. Clint pulled his left hand from its path before his fingers could be crushed. The team horses whinnied in fear. They had been trained to overcome gunshyness, but the buckshot must have come close enough to convince them that they were threatened. Yet the team didn't break into a frenzied gallop, and neither animal cried out in pain.

Clint glanced about. Duke had vanished, but the Gunsmith knew his prized Arabian had a highly developed survival instinct. Duke had an uncanny knack for locating the best shelter faster than any human Clint had ever known. That gelding gave a whole new meaning to the term "horse sense."

The Gunsmith scanned the area for any other drygulchers who might be lying in wait. This time it didn't seem to be an organized attack with snipers employing a crossfire. Maybe Huntington-Smythe's men weren't responsible.

Suddenly the reports of two rapid-fire rifle shots echoed from the rock walls above. Clint spotted a figure on a cliff. The rifleman worked the lever of his weapon and fired another round at the shotgunner's position.

"Hello, below!" a voice shouted from the rock wall. "You can come out now. We drove that bastard off!"

"How do I know you're not just trying to trick me into exposing myself so you can gun me down?" the Gunsmith called out in reply.

"Wouldn't have no reason to want a do that, Mr. Adams," the voice answered. "You're Clint Adams, ain't you?"

"That's right," Clint admitted. "So what?"

"I'm Stan Struthers. Don't reckon you remember me. I was with Johnny Hacker when you rode up on that big black hoss this morning."

"I remember you, Stan," the Gunsmith told the voice. "What's going on here?"

"Feller tried to kill you, Clint." Stan's voice contained a chuckle. "Figured you would have noticed that."

"You're saying that guy with the shotgun isn't one of your men?" Clint asked.

"If'n we'd wanted you dead, we would have shot at you instead of him."

"That makes sense," the Gunsmith admitted. "We're gonna shout ourselves hoarse if we keep this up. Why don't you fellas come on down and I'll set up camp. We can talk about this over a pot of coffee."

"That's to my taste," Stan declared. "We'll take you up on that offer, Clint."

Stan Struthers, the short stocky cowhand Clint had

met briefly earlier that day, was a subcommander under John Hacker. He and another member of Huntington-Smythe's gunhawks climbed down from the rocks to join the Gunsmith as Clint built a campfire and started to prepare the coffee.

"Howdy, Clint," Stan greeted, canting a Spencer carbine over his shoulder as he approached the camp. "Don't think you met Harry afore."

"Howdy, Mr. Adams," Harry, a tall waspy cowboy said, tucking his Winchester under his arm.

"I'm obliged to you gents for helping me," the Gunsmith told them.

"Don't reckon the major would be too happy with us if'n we let some bushwhacker gun you down." Stan shrugged. "He was purely pissed about Pierce and Thomlen jumpin' you the other day."

"I figure this makes up for that incident," Clint assured him.

Duke emerged from the side of a boulder he'd used for cover during the firefight. The gelding neighed curtly at Clint. Duke extended his neck and snorted twice.

"Okay, okay," Clint rolled his eyes toward heaven. "You tried to warn me and I should have listened to you. What do you want? A medal?"

Duke's ears twitched as he stared at Clint, as if he was seriously considering the question.

"What the hell would you do with a medal?" The Gunsmith smiled. "Come on. I'll give you some sugar instead."

Stan and Harry were dumbfounded as they watched the gelding trot over to Clint. The Gunsmith patted Duke's neck and gave him two cubes of sugar. The horse nodded his head as he crunched the treat in his teeth.

"Glad you like it." Clint grinned. "See? Even you couldn't eat a medal, big fella."

"Golly be damned," Harry remarked numbly. "That hoss thinks he's a human being!"

"What horse are you talking about?" the Gunsmith asked, managing to keep a straight face.

"Never mind," Harry replied, shaking his head.

"Coffee will be a spell," Clint announced. "You fellas care for a shot of whiskey while you're waiting on it?"

"That'd be plum generous." Stan nodded. "I'm glad to see you trusted us to come into your camp peaceable."

"Well, I don't see that you'd have any reason to try to kill me," the Gunsmith stated. "Besides, when you fellas accepted my invitation you came down here within pistol range. If you did try anything, I'd have a better chance of dealing with it on my terms."

"No need to fret, Clint," Stan assured him. "We got no quarrel with you. Neither does Huntington-Smythe."

"But that big jasper with the shotgun is another story," Harry declared.

"Did you get a good look at him?" Clint asked.

"Can't say I did." Harry shrugged. "Fella kept pretty much covered by the rock rubble. I could tell he was a big bastard. More'n six feet tall and built like a Mex fightin' bull."

"When we seen you was in trouble," Stan added, "we took a few shots at the drygulcher. Figured we could flush 'im out and wing him with a bullet. Feller took off, sure enough. Trouble is he got through an archway of natural rock what leads to the gorge beyond. He's probably limped off to the middle of the pine forest by now."

"Limped?" Clint raised his eyebrows. "Did one of your bullets wound him?"

"Can't say for certain." Stan shrugged. "But I don't think so. Probably just twisted his ankle runnin' across the rocks."

"Maybe," the Gunsmith said. "Or he might still be recovering from a kick to the balls."

"How's that?" Stan asked.

"I had a fight with a big man before I left Dublin," Clint explained. "Fella might have decided to get even."

"That means he's doubled back and headed for town," Harry mused. "Pity we didn't know that, or we could have cut him off by now."

"He's not important," the Gunsmith stated. "You fellas know Huntington-Smythe pretty well. You figure he'd listen if I explained a couple things about Dublin?"

"Reckon so," Stan answered. "You plan on payin' the major another visit?"

"Yeah," the Gunsmith replied. "Right after we've had our coffee."

NINETEEN

"You seem to be quite a lightning rod, Mr. Adams," Huntington-Smythe commented as he escorted the Gunsmith into the dining room. "I've never see a man so adept at attracting trouble."

"Everybody has a sort of natural talent for something," Clint replied with a shrug.

"Indeed." The Briton smiled, polishing his monocle with a silk handkerchief. "I took the liberty of telling Christine to set a place for you at the table. I trust you're hungry, Mr. Adams."

"That's very kind of you, Major," the Gunsmith said. "I've been so busy today I hardly took time to have some beef jerky and sourdough bread this morning. A real sit-down dinner sounds mighty fine. Thank you."

"You're quite welcome," Huntington-Smythe assured him. "You will of course stay here tonight and have breakfast before you leave."

"I couldn't impose on your hospitality . . ." Clint began.

"Nonsense," the major replied. "The sun has already set and it will be quite dark by the time we finish dinner. I would be remiss as a host to offer you less, Mr. Adams."

• • •

The dining room was pleasant, with walnut furniture and a white cloth draped over the table. Huntington-Smythe sat at its head. John Hacker's seat was to his left, and a heavyset man with a dense black beard and a nose which resembled a bent doorknob sat at the major's right.

"I'm certain you remember Mr. Hacker," Huntington-Smythe declared. "This other gentleman is Hamilton Jones, my foreman and chief engineer at the mines."

"Pleasure to meet you," Clint said.

"Yeah," Jones muttered.

"Didn't figure I'd be seein' you again so soon," Hacker told Clint. "Reckon you'd best stay clear of that damn ravine."

"Now you tell me." The Gunsmith grinned.

Christine, the lovely maid, entered and served the meal. With roast beef, boiled potatoes, buttered corn on the cob and red wine in front of him, the Gunsmith had to remind himself why he'd returned to the major's spread.

"All right, Mr. Adams," Huntington-Smythe remarked as he sipped his wine, "I'm certain you didn't come here simply to tell me you were attacked by a shotgun-wielding Irishman."

"No, sir," Clint admitted.

"I see." The Briton smiled. "Perhaps you're here in search of employment. If you want to offer your skills, I'll be happy to hire you. Lord knows you're well qualified."

"That's a fact," Hacker confirmed.

"I'm not looking for a job, Major," the Gunsmith said. "I wanted to tell you that I think you're right about the Molly Maguires being involved in the problems you've had recently."

"Indeed." Huntington-Smythe cocked his head to one side. "And why do you say that?"

"I asked a few questions in Dublin," Clint began. "And I pushed a couple suspects a little. Two of them pushed back. You want the details?"

"I really don't like to discuss the Irish while I'm eating," the Briton replied. "Actually, Mr. Adams, I already knew they were responsible for dynamiting that mine shaft, and there could be no doubt whatsoever about their attack on my men. You really haven't told me anything I didn't already know."

"Did you know the man your guards killed was a sacrifice by the Molly Maguires?" the Gunsmith inquired.

"A sacrifice?" The Briton frowned. "Why would they want us to kill one of their own men?"

"Malloy, the man your guards shot, wasn't a Molly," Clint explained. "The Mollies got him drunk and suckered him into joining them for what he thought was a practical joke. They wanted Malloy to die."

"That dead man sure smelled of liquor," Hacker confirmed.

"*All* Irishmen smell that way," Huntington-Smythe said dryly. "I repeat my question, Mr. Adams. Why?"

"To serve as a martyr," Clint answered.

"Horse shit." Jones sneered as he chewed a mouthful of beef.

"Remember the Boston Massacre?" the Gunsmith asked. "Seven guys threw snowballs at British troops. The soldiers shot them down. Now, at first, everybody felt those fellas were just troublemakers and nobody got too upset about their deaths. Not even the Colonials in New England cared. But when the war got hot, those seven guys became heroes. You can get a lot of folks fired up over a good martyr or two."

The Briton sighed. "What's your point?"

"The Molly Maguires are trying to incite a war between Dublin and your forces, Major," Clint replied. "Just three men are responsible for this. Not the entire town."

"But the rest of the population certainly realizes these men are Molly Maguires," Huntington-Smythe said.

"You can't blame everybody in Dublin for what three men might do," Clint insisted.

"But they *all* know about those three men, correct?"

"I think most of the town suspects the trio were Mollies back East," the Gunsmith admitted. "But they don't realize the Mollies are active here."

"Of course they realize it, Mr. Adams," the Briton stated. "But they don't see anything wrong with murder and destruction as long as it is done by Irishmen. Especially if the victims are British."

"And you don't see anything wrong with punishing everybody in Dublin because they're Irish," Clint told him.

Huntington-Smythe glared at Clint. "Do you make a habit of insulting a man in his own house, Mr. Adams?"

"I didn't mean to sound rude, Major," Clint assured him. "But this is a serious matter, and a lot of lives might depend on how you react in the future."

"I say we go down there and run them Micks outta the state of Colorado," Jones declared gruffly.

"Lucky you ain't in charge, Ham," Hacker muttered.

"Oh, yeah?" Jones growled. "What do you care about those mines, Hacker? You gunfighters ain't got homes or families to worry about. All you care about is

DYNAMITE JUSTICE   119

gettin' your money for guarding the major's property. Longer the Irish present a threat, the better you like it."

"Those folks ain't gonna move without a fight," Hacker replied. "That what you want?"

"What I want is to see those mines earns a profit that'll make two years of back-breakin' work worthwhile," Jones told him. "You weren't here when we started workin' those hills, Hacker. You don't know how hard it was to get those shafts built and start haulin' out the coal. We've been short-handed from the start and still need to hire more men. Now we can afford to. Those hills are gonna make the major a rich man, and those of us workin' for him will profit as well."

"If you need men," Clint began, "why did you refuse to hire the Irishmen who came here looking for jobs?"

"That should be obvious," Huntington-Smythe said. "Do you think I'd risk letting members of the Molly Maguires or the Fenians into my mines?"

"Most of the men in Dublin aren't Mollies," Clint said.

"It only takes one to light a fuse to a bundle of dynamite. Irishmen in an Englishman's mine is inviting destruction, Mr. Adams," Huntington-Smythe said stiffly.

"Maybe if the Irish weren't treated like dirt there wouldn't be criminal outfits like the Molly Maguires," the Gunsmith commented. "Or at least they wouldn't find support and sympathy from the rest of the Irish community."

"You sure got a smart mouth on you, Adams," Jones growled.

"Smarter than your whole body, Jones."

"I don't care if'n you are a big bad gunfighter,"

Jones hissed as he began to rise from his chair. "I've a mind to beat the shit out of you, Adams . . ."

"Sit down," Huntington-Smythe ordered. "I'll not have this conversation degenerate into a brawl. Both of you are getting verbally offensive, and I'd thank you both to remain civil while you are at this table."

"I apologize for my rudeness," the Gunsmith declared. "But Mr. Jones knows what the Irish miners have experienced back East. The coal mines are black, damp holes filled with black dust. Miners work in those pits until their hands are raw and their nails are caked with coal dust and blood. That soot gets in their lungs. Every evening you can hear them coughing after they leave the mines.

"And what do the miners get for their labors?" Clint continued. "They get to live in flimsy shacks at the base of the hills where the mines are located. They freeze in the winter and boil in the summer. They get to raise their families in filth, despair and ignorance. Who can afford to send their children to school when they only make a few pennies every month?"

"Coal miners are paid better wages than that," Huntington-Smythe stated.

"But money is taken out of a coal miner's salary for goods from the company stores," Clint corrected. "Goods that are always overpriced because the companies realize their customers can't get supplies any other way, unless they're willing to travel thirty or forty miles to the nearest town. Can you blame the Irish for feeling trapped and abused? Can you really be surprised that some of them have chosen to respond to such treatment with anger and violence?"

"You seem to know a great deal about the coal mines of Pennsylvania, Mr. Adams," the Briton remarked.

"I'm from the East originally," the Gunsmith answered. "I've seen it for myself. That's why I can sympathize with the coal miners, but I don't approve of the Molly Maguires. Their violent tactics might be drawing public attention to the conditions of the mines, but they're hurting a lot of innocent people in the process. And I'm afraid a lot of innocent folks will get hurt here if you and the people of Dublin don't try to live peaceably together."

"What do you suggest?" Huntington-Smythe inquired.

"Meet with the mayor, Sean O'Hara, and talk to him about the possibility of hiring some of the townsfolk as miners," Clint began. "Mr. Jones seems quite loyal to you, Major, and I believe you are basically a fair man who wouldn't submit his employees to the types of conditions common to the mines back East."

"Thank you for that much, Mr. Adams." The Briton smiled. "But what if I wind up with Molly Maguire saboteurs in my mines?"

"I'll talk to O'Hara about the three guys who are almost certainly Molly Maguires," the Gunsmith explained. "He'll have to agree that those three won't be included among the men you hire. Or that they'll have to expect to be searched and strictly supervised within the mines."

"Why not simply insist that the trio be run out of town?" Hacker suggested.

"Because the town is sympathetic toward them," Clint explained. "And they don't like the British. Now, if an Englishman was to offer them a fair deal and proved to be a man of his word, then the Molly Maguires could cry about past injustice until they were blue in the face. The rest of the Irish would realize those three were just troublemakers and tell the Mollies to go to hell."

"I notice you've been careful not to mention the names of these offenders," Hacker remarked.

"That's right," Clint confessed. "I don't want to take the chance that you fellas might decide to just ride into Dublin and demand that they turn over those three men to you. That would trigger a shootin' war for sure."

"I don't want that to happen," Huntington-Smythe stated. "That's the reason I tried to cut off supplies to Dublin—to drive them out without bloodshed."

"I appreciate that." The Gunsmith nodded. "I also realize you could easily overpower the Irish and wipe out Dublin. You've got plenty of experienced gunmen on your payroll, and a good commander for them with John Hacker here."

Hacker grinned. "Thanks for the compliment."

"If this can be handled peaceably I'm willing to make the first move," Huntington-Smythe confirmed. "You meet with O'Hara, Mr. Adams. If he agrees to all our terms, we'll see if we can work this out."

"Thank you, Major," the Gunsmith replied.

"However," the Briton added, "if this doesn't work, or if the Irish launch another attack on the mines, I may have to resort to a full-scale siege."

"I thought you didn't want bloodshed," Clint remarked.

"I don't, Mr. Adams," Huntington-Smythe assured him. "But if it has to happen, I'd rather the Irish do the bleeding than my men. For everyone's sake, I certainly hope your plan proves successful."

TWENTY

The following morning, Clint Adams drove his wagon from Huntington-Smythe's property and headed back toward Dublin. John Hacker had suggested that a couple of his men might escort the wagon in case the renegade assassin made another attempt to kill the Gunsmith. Clint had refused the offer because the Irish would be alarmed if they saw him ride up with a couple of the Englishman's troops.

The Gunsmith carried his .45-caliber Springfield across his lap in case of an ambush as he held the reins lightly in his left fist. His right hand rested on the frame of his carbine. Clint glanced about, leery of possible danger.

Yet the Gunsmith considered it unlikely that he'd be attacked again. The shotgun killer must have been Mike O'Quinn. The big Irishman would have returned to Dublin after Stan and Harry drove him off. He'd probably be reluctant to attempt another ambush on the trail, and he'd have no reason to think the Gunsmith would return to the town. Still, Clint didn't want to be taken off guard again.

The Gunsmith felt good about his mission as a go-between for a peace agreement between Dublin and Huntington-Smythe's camp. More often than not,

Clint found himself in a situation that he was forced to shoot his way out of. It would be a pleasant change to solve a problem with words instead of bullets.

"Well, so much for my notion about minding my own business and not getting involved with other folks' troubles." Clint sighed. "Reckon I'm getting too old to be serious about changing my ways now."

Duke snorted loudly as he tagged along at the rear of the wagon. Clint rolled his eyes and turned to call back at the gelding, "I know, you told me so, right?"

Then he noticed something move among his gear in the back of the wagon. Clint instantly thrust the barrel of his Springfield through the canvas opening and aimed it at the humanoid shadow inside the rig.

"Hands up or I'll put a bullet right through your head," Clint declared harshly.

"Please, don't shoot me, Mr. Adams," a feminine voice replied timidly.

"What the hell?" the Gunsmith wondered in surprise. "Come out of there."

He pulled the reins to bring the wagon to a full stop. The girl emerged from the interior, both hands still held at shoulder level to reveal she wasn't armed. Clint lowered his carbine and took Christine's arm to help her climb into the seat next to him.

"What the hell were you doing back there?" he demanded.

"I sneaked into your wagon after breakfast," she replied. "Nobody noticed me when you hitched the rig to your team . . ."

"I guess they didn't," Clint remarked. "But I kinda doubt anybody was looking for you then. Huntington-Smythe is certainly looking for you by now, and I don't think he'll be very happy when he finds out you stowed away in my wagon."

"I didn't mean to get you in trouble, sir," the girl said sadly. "But I had to get out of there somehow."

"I wasn't aware Huntington-Smythe was holding you there against your will." The Gunsmith frowned.

"We had an agreement," she explained. "I was educated in an orphanage in Maryland, but I wanted to come to the West to sort of start over. I met the major in a hotel in Baltimore where I was working as a maid. We talked about the West. When he learned I wanted to come out here, he made me an offer."

The Gunsmith frowned, but remained silent.

"Do you know what an indentured servant is?" Christine asked. "It means that a person is contracted to work for someone to repay a debt. Well, I became the major's indentured servant. I became his maid, his mistress, his property."

"How long was this contract for?" Clint asked.

"Two years," Christine answered. "My indentured labor period expired three months ago."

"But Huntington-Smythe wouldn't let you leave?"

"He said he didn't want to let me go until he was certain the problems with the Irish were over. Afraid I'd be kidnapped or something."

"Sounds like he cares about you some."

"Fond of me like one might be of a pet cat."

"Has he treated you badly?" Clint asked.

"That depends on what you mean," Christine answered. "I wasn't starved or beaten. What bothered me most was being treated like a whore, forced to sleep with an older man. Silly really, because the major doesn't have much interest in love-making. We haven't—uh—indulged for over six months."

"Well, not all older men are over the hill," Clint commented, aware that Huntington-Smythe was probably no older than himself.

"I just want to be free, sir," Christine pleaded. "Please don't take me back there."

"Calm down," Clint urged. "I'm not going to make you do anything you don't want to do."

"Oh, thank you!"

Christine suddenly wrapped her arms around his neck and kissed him. The Gunsmith naturally returned her embrace. His mouth pressed against hers, lingering in the sweet taste of her lips. Clint's tongue entered her mouth, stroking the interior tenderly.

The girl's boldness startled him. She slid her hands over his body as they kissed. Fingers probed between his legs, caressing him. The Gunsmith squeezed her breasts in reply, feeling her nipples stiffen under his touch.

"I haven't had a man for so long," Christine whispered in a husky, passionate voice.

"Be happy to take care of that for you," Clint assured her. "But right now isn't such a good time for . . ."

"Oh?" the girl smiled. "Maybe I can change your mind about that."

Christine moved her fingers to the fabric of her dark blue dress. Slowly, she raised the skirt. The hemline rose above her knees. Christine hiked the skirt up to her thighs. Clint stared at the long, shapely naked limbs. She held the skirt up to her hips to reveal the dark triangle between her beautiful legs.

"You sure know how to convince a fella," Clint told her.

He ran his fingers along the warm smooth flesh of her thighs. Christine's hand moved to Clint's crotch and unbuttoned his trousers. The Gunsmith unbuckled his gunbelt as the girl began to pull his pants down.

Soon Clint was naked from the waist down. Only the cloth of his shirttail protected his backside from the coarse wooden bench. Christine climbed into his lap and straddled him like a horse. Clint held her skirt up while the girl eased herself onto the top of his erect penis.

Clint felt himself sink into the warm, damp chamber. Christine gripped him like a hot, tight fist. She wiggled against Clint, working him deeper. The Gunsmith placed his mouth on her breasts. He gently chewed and sucked them through the cloth of her dress.

The girl slowly began to raise and lower herself along the length of his stiff cock. She crooned happily and increased the motion. Clint arched his back to meet her thrusts, driving himself in farther.

Christine gasped breathlessly and rode his shaft faster. Suddenly she gripped his thighs with her knees. Her body trembled as a passionate climax flowed through her.

The Gunsmith's throbbing penis erupted inside her like a miniature volcano. He sighed with pleasure as he blasted his seed into Christine's womanhood. She gasped in even greater pleasure when she felt the hot pulse throb between her splayed legs.

"Oh, that was wonderful," the girl said, snuggling against Clint's chest.

"I'm eager to see what we can do when we've got a bed and plenty of time for making love," the Gunsmith told her. "But right now I've got to—"

The roar of an explosion interrupted his sentence.

They turned toward the sound and saw a cloud of dust and rock debris rise from the base of a hill in the distance.

"That's where the mines are located," Christine declared.

"Oh, shit," Clint hissed through his teeth. "The fat's in the fire for sure now."

TWENTY-ONE

"Stay here," the Gunsmith instructed as he pulled up his pants.

"Where would I go?" Christine replied with a shrug.

Clint buckled on his gunbelt and grabbed the Springfield in one hand and his Dolland with the other. The Gunsmith jumped down from the rig and headed for a cluster of boulders. A confused Christine watched with alarm.

"Hey, where are you going?" she called to him.

"Just want a better look," he replied as he scrambled up the rocks. "I'll be right back. Promise."

The Gunsmith scaled the stony pile rapidly. He climbed to the summit and opened the pocket telescope to full length. Clint gazed through the Dolland and scanned the area surrounding the base of the hill where the dust had yet to settle.

Several figures stirred near the mouth of a mine. Soot still drifted from the tunnel like smoke from the open jaws of a great stone dragon. The men clustered around the dusty mist were dressed in gray coveralls and miners' helmets. One of Hacker's gunmen, clad in denim and a stetson, darted forward to investigate.

Then three men emerged from the dust clouds. Like

the miners, they wore gray coveralls, but their heads were encased in white flour sacks with holes for their eyes. All of them carried pistols.

The trio opened fire. Clint saw the sentry convulse as bullets crashed into his body. The unarmed miners pivoted and tried to flee. The three masked gunmen took aim and fired again. Two miners tumbled to the ground with bullets in thir backs.

"Goddamn butchers," the Gunsmith hissed helplessly, aware that the killers were out of range. There was nothing he could do except stand by and witness the slaughter.

Despite the masks, Clint had no doubt about the identity of the three killers. One man was large and muscular, another short and wiry, and the third was of medium height with a lean waist and a powerful upper torso.

The trio allowed the rest of the miners to escape. Then they bolted around the edge of the hill. Clint scrambled down the rocks and leaped to the ground. He whistled sharply. Duke replied with a loud neigh. The powerful gelding grabbed the guideline in his teeth and pulled hard, snapping the rope.

Duke galloped forward to meet the Gunsmith. Clint caught the horse's reins in one hand, shoving the Springfield into the rifle boot attached to the saddle. The Gunsmith grabbed the horn and hauled himself up.

"Where are you going now?" Christine asked, both confused and concerned.

"Just saw three killers," Clint replied. "Gonna try to cut them off before they can get back to Dublin."

"What am I supposed to do?" she asked.

"Just wait for me, okay?"

"If you'll make me a promise," Christine replied.

"What sort of promise?" he asked.

"That you won't get yourself killed."

"Not much chance of that," Clint assured her. "Don't worry. This shouldn't take long."

The Gunsmith urged Duke into a gallop. The gelding had had little exercise for the last few days and he eagerly responded, glad for a chance to stretch his legs. Clint rode along the dirt road until he could cut across the prairie toward the mining hills.

Clint spotted three figures on horseback galloping for the treeline of a pinewood forest. The trio still wore the flour sacks over their heads. At least the Gunsmith was certain he was following the right men.

The trio yanked off their masks as they neared the trees. The hoods would have restricted their peripheral vision, which was vital for rapid movement through the forest. Clint pulled Duke's reins to the right, steering the big gelding toward the fleeing terrorists.

Suddenly, two pistol shots cracked. Clint brought Duke to a halt and leaped from the saddle. He wrapped his arms around the horse's neck, shoving a hand against Duke's jawbone. The gelding recalled his training and bent all four legs to lower himself to the ground.

"Good boy," Clint praised his horse, glad Duke had remembered a trick which he hadn't practiced for months.

The gelding lay on his side and placed his head and neck to the ground. The Gunsmith drew the Springfield carbine from its boot and told Duke to stay put. Then he lay prone and aimed the gun at the treeline.

A bullet ripped into the earth less than a foot from Clint's right elbow. Dirt splattered his shirt as he heard the report of a rifle. The Gunsmith instantly realized the shot had come from the rear. He rolled over and swung the carbine in that direction.

"Hold your fire!" John Hacker cried out. "It's Clint!"

Hacker and two other gunmen from Huntington-Smythe's spread rode toward the Gunsmith. Two of them held rifles ready. They stopped their horses near Clint as he rose to his feet.

"You happen to see three fellers wearin' hoods, Clint?" Hacker demanded.

"They fled into the trees," Clint replied. "Don't go after them. They've got too much cover in there. They'll cut you guys down before you get a clear target to shoot at."

"Can't just let 'em get away," Hacker stated. "Done killed at least four men. Maybe more. Won't know for sure until they've dug open the mineshaft."

"The explosion was inside the shaft?" the Gunsmith asked.

"Yeah," Hacker confirmed. "And there was men workin' in there, too."

"How does Adams know 'bout that explosion?" one of the gunhawks inquired, his eyes narrowed with suspicion.

"Probably heard it, Bob," Hacker replied. "Weren't exactly quiet, now was it?"

"Also got a look at the mine with my spyglass," the Gunsmith told them. "Saw the killers gun down three of your men in cold blood. Shot the miners in the back when they tried to run for cover."

"I know," Hacker nodded grimly. "They also knifed one of our sentries. Major's gonna want blood for sure, Clint. Can't say as I blame him neither."

"Look," the Gunsmith urged. "You guys don't

want to swoop down on Dublin and massacre the whole town—"

"Reckon that's where we'll be headin', Clint." Hacker shrugged. "Since them killers haven't fired a shot from the forest, it's a safe bet they've moved on for home. I'm going back to the major and report to him. Reckon we both know what he'll want to do."

"I'm going to Dublin now," Clint explained. "Give me an hour—"

"Ain't up to me, Clint," Hacker told him. "The major will decide. Figure we'll need a while to dig out those fellers trapped in the mineshaft. After that's finished, you can bet your ass we'll ride to Dublin."

"Try to get me as much time as possible," Clint urged. "Maybe I can explain things to the Irish."

"Don't do it, Clint," Hacker advised. "If you're in that town when we come there in force, you'll be smack dab in the middle of any shootin' that might occur. Reckon you know those Irish folks ain't gonna be apt to surrender, so we're probably gonna have a hell of a shoot-out. Hate to think of you being caught in a mess like that."

"Me too, John," the Gunsmith admitted. "But I'm going to have to live with myself for the rest of my life. I figure that might not be so easy if I just ride on without doing everything in my power to try to stop you folks from killing each other."

"Seems to me you've done enough already, Clint." Hacker sighed. "If'n you insist on tryin' to do more, I reckon that's your funeral."

"Well"—the Gunsmith smiled weakly—"I kinda hope it doesn't come to that."

TWENTY-TWO

"Holy Saint Patrick!" Duffy exclaimed when the Gunsmith's wagon rolled to the mouth of the livery stable. "Sure'n I never expected to see you again, Clint."

"Didn't plan on coming back," the Gunsmith replied. "But something happened to change my mind."

"Who's the lady?" Duffy asked, grinning at Christine. "Another friend of yours?"

"What does that mean?" the girl asked Clint.

"Nothing," Clint said. "Duffy just has an odd sense of humor."

"Probably true." The hostler shrugged. "But then I'm Irish. Anyway, what can I do for you, Clint?"

"Look after my wagon and Christine while I have a talk with O'Hara," the Gunsmith answered as he climbed down from the rig.

"Be a pleasure," Duffy assured him. "But I suspect somethin' must be wrong for you to be comin' back here to see the mayor. Right?"

"You guessed it, friend," Clint confirmed.

"Trouble with the Englishman?" the old man inquired.

"Trouble has been coming from all directions," the Gunsmith replied. "From Dublin as well as the mines.

135

It's all been building up to a peak for a long time now. Looks like it's finally happened."

"Oh, Jesus," Duffy whispered. "We'd better get prepared . . ."

"You just relax until I've talked to O'Hara," Clint told him. "And don't talk to anyone about this until I come back."

"Okay, Clint." Duffy sighed. "But sure'n I hope you know what you be doin'."

"Me too," the Gunsmith admitted.

Clint walked to the home of Sean O'Hara and knocked on the door. No one replied. He wondered if O'Hara might be at the rear of the house, perhaps chopping wood or hauling water.

The Gunsmith moved to the back of the dwelling. He didn't see O'Hara or his wife Maureen. Then he heard two voices. The sound came from a window. A man and a woman groaned in passionate delight. Clint detected the creak of bedsprings among the moans.

"Oh, Sean," Maureen's voice gasped. "Don't stop, darling. Don't . . ."

"Don't worry, me dear," O'Hara's voice assured her. "This time we be on the way to Paradise together."

Clint Adams smiled. The Gunsmith returned to the front of the house and pounded on the door. Eventually, Sean O'Hara answered it. He was clad in a longjohn shirt and trousers and nothing else.

"Clint Adams," the Irishman said with surprise. "I thought you'd left town determined never to return to our backward little community."

"Your backward little community is going to be stomped into the ground if you don't listen to me, Sean," the Gunsmith said bluntly.

"What are you talkin' 'bout?" O'Hara demanded, moving aside to allow Clint to enter.

"Did you hear an explosion about half an hour ago?" Clint asked as he closed the door.

"Aye." O'Hara shrugged. "The Limey must be blasting a new tunnel or something."

"Huntington-Smythe didn't do the blasting," Clint explained. "The Molly Maguires did."

"Sweet Jesus," O'Hara moaned. "Is the Brit blamin' us for another bloody accident up there?"

"No accident," Clint declared. "I saw it, Sean. Three men wearing hoods killed some of Huntington-Smythe's people. Three Molly Maguires named Corrigan, Durkan and O'Quinn."

"You said they were wearing masks . . ." O'Hara began lamely.

"Shit," Clint snorted. "You know damn good and well I couldn't mistake those three for anybody else. They're all built so differently, the striking contrast of each man's size makes them unmistakable when they're together. Or do you intend to tell me it could just be a coincidence that one killer happens to be six and a half feet tall and built like a mountain, another is short and thin, and the third is built just like Jack Corrigan?"

"You still can't be sure—"

"I'm sure," the Gunsmith snapped. "And you'd better be concerned about protecting the innocent people in Dublin instead of covering up for the guilty."

"What do you mean?" O'Hara demanded.

"Huntington-Smythe is going to be here any minute, Sean," Clint warned. "You'd better tell your people not to aim a weapon at them. One person points a sling-shot at the Englishman's group and this town will be shot to pieces before you can say whiskey."

"You expect me to tell the people of this town to knuckle under to a Limey's threats?" O'Hara snorted. "We're Irish and—"

"Goddamn it!" Clint declared angrily. "I'm sick to death of hearing how the Irish and the English hate each other's guts. We're not talking about old grudges."

"No, we're talking about Huntington-Smythe," the Irishman snapped. "And you don't think we should fight the bastard?"

"Fight him?" The Gunsmith shook his head. "What the hell for? Huntington-Smythe wants the Molly Maguires. The rest of your people will only get hurt if they insist on protecting Corrigan and his men."

"Jesus, Clint," O'Hara began. "I don't know what to do."

"You just talk to your people," Clint replied as he headed for the door. "I'll take care of the other three."

TWENTY-THREE

The Glenmalure was closed. The front door of the saloon was locked and the shades to all the windows were drawn. Clint Adams tried to peer under the bottom of a window blind, but all he saw was the back of a chair.

Guess I'll find out what's in there when I get inside, the Gunsmith thought as he reached into a pocket.

Clint removed a slender leather packet which contained some fundamental gunsmithing tools. He opened it and selected two—a slim metal cartridge probe generally used to pry loose warped shell casings or remove broken springs and firing pins, and a slender hacksaw designed for delicate metal cutting.

Long ago, Clint had discovered these tools could serve more than one purpose. He carefully inserted the saw blade into the keyhole of the tavern door. Clint moved the flexible strip of metal slowly until its teeth caught on the tumblers inside the lock. Then he slid in the probe and worked both tools in unison. Ten seconds later, his efforts were rewarded by a single click within the door.

The Gunsmith put away his tools and placed his right hand on the grips of his holstered Colt revolver. He gripped the doorknob in his left hand and turned it slowly. Clint pushed the door open.

Jack Corrigan, Mike O'Quinn and Timothy Durkan were clustered together at the end of the bar, sharing a bottle of Irish whiskey. Apparently they were toasting success—either of the present or the future—when the Gunsmith entered the saloon.

"Oh, damn!" O'Quinn exclaimed with alarm when he saw Clint. A shot glass fell from his hand and shattered on the floor.

The big Irishman reached for the revolver thrust in his belt. The Gunsmith drew his Colt first. O'Quinn stared into the muzzle of Clint's pistol and immediately raised his hands. Corrigan and Durkan followed his example.

"Don't tell me you've decided to start robbin' taverns for a livin', Clint," Corrigan remarked, still maintaining his cool exterior. "I assure you this one hardly be worth your trouble, mate."

"Damn it, Timmy," O'Quinn growled at Durkan. "I thought you locked the bleedin' door!"

"I did, Mike," the little man insisted. "Sure as God be me witness, I did."

"Never mind that now," Clint began. "All of you, drop your guns. Move real slow. Just use one finger and a thumb to grip the gun at the butt. Then drop 'em and raise your hands."

"Well, we've not much choice in the matter," Corrigan commented. "But would you mind tellin' us what this is all 'bout?"

"It's about murder, sabotage and the Molly Maguires," the Gunsmith explained as he kicked the door shut and walked toward the trio.

Corrigan sighed. "The Molly Maguires again. You have no proof of such accusations. We've discussed this before—"

"You guys celebrating the fact you just blew up a mineshaft and killed several men in cold blood?" Clint asked.

"Nothin' of the sort, lad," Corrigan smiled. "We were just celebratin'—"

"I want O'Quinn to answer me," the Gunsmith insisted.

"Uh," the big man began awkwardly. "We were just havin' a friendly little drink is all."

"We're celebratin' our second month of runnin' the Glenmalure," Corrigan said quickly. "Isn't that right, lads?"

"Aye," Durkan agreed.

"Uh, aye," O'Quinn added. "That's right."

"I bet," the Gunsmith muttered. "Kick those guns over here."

All three men obeyed.

"Now face the bar and place your hands on the counter," Clint instructed. "Palms down."

The trio continued to follow orders. Clint bent over to pick up one of the revolvers. O'Quinn, the closest man, suddenly whirled and grabbed for the Gunsmith's wrist.

Clint pulled his right arm away from O'Quinn before the big man could seize it. The Gunsmith's left hand swung up from the floor. He held a pistol barrel in his fist and smashed the gunbutt across O'Quinn's jaw. The Irish brute crashed to the floor with a groan.

"Don't try it!" Clint warned the others, pointing his Colt at the pair.

"This is bloody nonsense, Clint," Corrigan snapped.

"Yeah," Clint growled. "I should have shot O'Quinn instead of just busting his jaw. You guys know O'Quinn tried to kill me with a shotgun earlier today?"

"You're wrong, Clint," Corrigan declared. "Mike has been with us ever since you thrashed him in that fist fight."

"And none of you left Dublin today?" Clint asked.

"That's right," Durkan replied angrily. "And you can't prove no different!"

Clint raised the revolver in his left hand and smelled the barrel. The pungent odor of burnt gunpowder assaulted his nostrils.

"This gun has been fired recently," he announced, placing the pistol on a nearby table. "I bet the other two have been, also."

He checked the two remaining pistols. All smelled of burnt gunpowder.

"No wonder you guys wouldn't take me up on that bet," he remarked.

"You'll need more proof than that, Clint," Corrigan stated calmly. "We did a bit of target shootin' today. No law against that. Is there?"

"Too bad for you guys," the Gunsmith said. "I saw you three at the mine. Almost caught up with you when you headed for the forest. Didn't you guys recognize me when you took those couple potshots?"

"Bullshit," Durkan snapped. "That wasn't us."

"I recognized you three," Clint told him.

"You saw three men wearing masks." Durkan sneered. "You couldn't recognize anybody, Adams!"

"Masks?" The Gunsmith smiled. "I didn't mention the fact that they were wearing masks. Hey, Corrigan! Your boy goofed. You'd better try to talk your way out of this. I can hardly wait to hear your explanation."

"I don't have to bother." Corrigan sighed. "This is

your word against ours, Clint. We're Irish and you aren't. In Dublin that makes quite a difference. Folks will believe us. Not you."

"We'll see about that, Jack," Clint said.

"I'm a bit disappointed in you, mate," Corrigan commented. "I had hoped you might understand why we did this, but I suppose that would be askin' too much of a man who never had Irish blood in his veins, or coal dust in his lungs."

"Why don't you explain it to me, Corrigan?"

"We've been forced to live under the yoke of British slavery for centuries," Corrigan answered. "Not only in Ireland, but here in America as well—"

"I've heard this sad tale before," Clint muttered. "None of it excuses what you've done."

"You'd feel differently if you'd worked in the coal mines under a British foreman in Pennsylvania," Corrigan told him. "The company manager was a Brit, too. Most of the police were Welsh. When we protested the terrible conditions and miserable wages we were ignored. When we tried to organize a march to the high-and-mighty manager's mansion, the Brits had their uniformed Welsh lackeys arrest us. More than once I received a bull's baton in me belly because I asked what charges he had against me."

Corrigan shook his head. "What's the use, Clint? You were born an American. You think the Constitution applies to everybody. But I'll tell you, we had no right to assembly and our right to petition was a bloody joke because nobody cared. Not the company, not the governor, not the bleedin' president. Did you know President Lincoln sent federal troops to Pennsylvania to try to maintain order when the Brits complained 'bout us uppity, unruly Irish trash?"

"I know you folks got a raw deal back there," Clint remarked. "But Huntington-Smythe isn't to blame for that."

"He's a Brit," Durkan stated. "That makes him our enemy. When we went to him to see about gettin' work in his mines, he refused us. The bastard needs experienced miners but he didn't want any Irish workin' for him."

"We've had to grovel for British mine companies long enough," Corrigan insisted. "Time we ran a coal mine of our own. Time Irishmen were workin' for other Irishmen instead of heartless tyrants who don't give a damn if'n our children be starvin' and our wives weep because every dream crumbles into dust."

"Who would be the Irishman in charge of this new system?" Clint inquired. "Naturally, it would be you, Jack Corrigan. Spare your fairy tale for anybody who'll listen to it. I still figure you're looking for money and the power it buys, Corrigan. If you took command of the mining operation in this town, you'd be as bad, or worse, than any of those evil landlords who have oppressed the Irish in the past."

"That's a lie!" Durkan snapped. "Jack would never let no harm come to a fellow Irishman—"

"Tell that to Malloy, you idiot," Clint replied. "You noble Molly Maguires killed him as surely as if you'd pulled the trigger."

"We had to do that to get this town involved, damn it," Corrigan declared. "They're too soft and lazy. They're afraid to claim what's justly ours. Aye, *ours*. We've earned that mine because we sweated enough blood in the past adiggin' coal for the Brits. The rest of this town doesn't have the guts or the brains to do this. We have. If the others want to follow our example, so be it. If they want to run like frightened dogs, they're welcome to do that too."

"That's really great, Corrigan." Clint clucked his tongue with disgust. "You've given this entire town an opportunity to die for *your* cause. Huntington-Smythe and his men are probably going to hit Dublin to settle a score with these people for what you've done."

"Maybe that's what it'll take to wake these louts up and get them to fight," Corrigan replied.

"There isn't going to be any fight, Jack," the Gunsmith told him. "You three are going to pay for your crimes and—"

The unexpected roar of several gunshots in unison interrupted him. Another salvo of shots followed. Outside, women and children cried out in terror. Men cursed and shouted orders. Clint heard the ominous *click-clack* of a rifle lever preparing the weapon to fire.

The siege had begun.

TWENTY-FOUR

"You're too late, Adams," Corrigan announced. "The fight has bloody well started."

"You sound happy about it, you bastard," Clint said, amazed by the Irishman's attitude.

"That's because we can win, man," Corrigan answered. "Timmy Durkan is the best powderman this side of the bleedin' ocean and you're the best gunfighter in the West. If you'll join us, it'll even the odds."

"Christ," the Gunsmith muttered. "You're crazy, Corrigan."

"No," the Molly Maguire commander insisted. "You be daft if you can't see the opportunity I'm offerin' you. After we take over the mines, there'll be a lot of coal coming out of those hills. We'll make the profit on that coal, Clint. Think on that. A full partnership in a mining company. You won't have to dig out an ounce of coal or even help us manage the business. Just help us beat the Limey and—"

"I've heard enough, Corrigan," Clint told him. "Let's go before—"

Mike O'Quinn suddenly rose up from the floor. His broken jaw hung awkwardly on a dislocated hinge and blood trickled from the side of his mouth. Even so, he lunged at Clint like a drunken bear.

The Gunsmith sidestepped the clumsy attack. O'Quinn's groping fingers missed once again. Clint lashed the barrel of his Colt across the big man's skull. Mike O'Quinn fell on his face and didn't stir.

Timothy Durkan's boot rose. A sharp pain shot through the Gunsmith's hand when the little Irishman kicked the gun out of his grasp. Durkan smiled and held up his balled fists in a pugilist position.

"You little shit," Clint muttered as he raised his fists. "You saw what I did to O'Quinn, and now—"

Durkan moved like summer lightning. His left fist jabbed twice, hitting Clint in the breastbone and the point of the chin. The Gunsmith staggered backward. Durkan followed him and clipped Clint on the side of the jaw with a fast right cross.

"Keep him busy, Tim," Corrigan instructed.

"Aye," Durkan replied as he squared off once more.

The Gunsmith hadn't expected little Durkan to be a boxer. The diminutive Irishman didn't hit as hard as O'Quinn, but he was a hell of a lot faster and was a better pugilist. Durkan shuffled toward Clint and shot out another fast left.

The Gunsmith blocked the punch with his right forearm. Durkan's fist hit Clint's arm, bounced off and swooped into a sly left hook. Knuckles cracked against the side of Clint's head.

Durkan rammed a right uppercut to Clint's stomach. The Gunsmith didn't intend to fight the little pugilist on his terms. Clint used his greater size and weight. He wrapped his left arm around Durkan's neck before the Irishman could dance out of range.

Clint pulled him closer and drove a knee into Durkan's groin then hit the little man in the gut. Durkan gasped breathlessly, but still responded by delivering two short, stinging punches under the Gunsmith's ribcage. Both men staggered toward the bar, grappling, punching and trying to butt each other in the face.

Their foreheads met like a pair of dueling rams. Clint stumbled into the bar. His skull felt as if he'd been hit with an axe handle. Durkan was also dazed by the butting contest. He weaved unsteadily for a moment and then snarled before he attacked once more.

The Gunsmith dodged a left jab and blocked a right cross with his forearm. At last he got a clear target and swung a right cross of his own at Durkan's chin. The little man lifted his left shoulder and Clint's fist bounced off his shoulder muscle.

Durkan nailed Clint on the jaw with a solid right. The blow knocked the Gunsmith back into the bar. He pushed himself away from the counter only to catch another left hook which spun him around. Clint tasted blood as his belly hit against the bar.

A vicious punch landed just above Clint's right kidney. Another hit him in the small of the back. Durkan hammered the bottom of a fist between Clint's shoulder blades and followed with a punch to the left kidney. If he could rupture one of Clint's kidneys, the Gunsmith would be out of the fight. If he could damage both, Clint would probably die from internal bleeding.

The Gunsmith bellowed in pain and anger as he suddenly bent his right elbow, delivering a desperate backward slash. The point of his elbow crashed into Durkan's mouth. Two front teeth broke under the impact of the blow.

Durkan staggered backward. Clint whirled and

whipped a wild left hook to his opponent's face. Durkan's head turned violently, blood and spittle spewing from his torn lips.

Clint drove a right uppercut to Durkan's solar plexus. The smaller man's body jackknifed from the punch. Clint's left hand seized Durkan's shirt front as he pumped two more punches to the nerve center under the Irishman's chest.

Durkan doubled up with a choking gasp. Vomit poured from his open mouth. Clint shook his left hand to toss off some puke. His own stomach threatened to turn, but he ignored it. The Gunsmith quickly grabbed Durkan by the hair and yanked his head down.

Clint bent a knee and slammed it into Durkan's face. The little man's body went limp as if all his bones had suddenly dissolved. The Gunsmith released his opponent and allowed Durkan's unconscious body to fall to the barroom floor.

Then victory exploded in a tidal wave of pain.

The Gunsmith felt something hard crash into the back of his skull. He heard glass shatter and felt something sharp bite into his scalp. Then everything seemed to cease, and Clint Adams fell into a senseless black pit. . . .

TWENTY-FIVE

"Clint!" a voice called from the edge of oblivion. "Come on, Clint!"

The Gunsmith's first sensation was of a terrible, sharp pain inside his skull. Then he was aware that the dark womb that encased him was violently moving to and fro. He wanted to rest. Hell, couldn't they just let a man get some sleep?

"Damnation, lad!" the voice bellowed. "You've got to be gettin' up!"

Clint managed to peel open his heavy eyelids to see a shadowy figure towering above him. The shape raised a hand and swatted the palm across Clint's face. The slap struck a bruise and caused yet another sharp pain to stab at the Gunsmith's nervous system.

He angrily shoved the shadow, trying to throw a punch at his tormentor. The figure cried out in alarm and tumbled away from Clint. The Gunsmith shook his head to clear it. Two shards of glass fell from his hair.

Suddenly, the mist cleared. Clint's vision returned, along with the memories of recent events. His tormentor sat on the floor beside him. Duffy glared at Clint with more annoyance than anger or fear.

"Sure'n it be time you got off your ass, man," the old hostler complained.

"Corrigan and the others," Clint began, glancing around the barroom. Several chairs and tables lay on their sides and broken glass littered the floor. "They got away?"

"Don't see 'em, do you?" Duffy asked.

"Not now," the Gunsmith grunted as he tried to get to his feet. He fell back on his rump. "Shit."

"I'll give you a hand," the old man offered. "Looks like Corrigan and his lads worked you over pretty bad."

"Corrigan hit me," Clint stated as Duffy hauled him upright. "At least I think that's what happened. Pretty sure I'd knocked the other two unconscious."

"Figure somebody busted a bottle over your noggin," Duffy remarked. "Nasty cut from the looks of your head."

"I'll live," Clint assured him. "What about Huntington-Smythe?"

"The Briton has the town surrounded," Duffy answered. "His men fired warnin' shots to force everybody to run for cover. That's how I wound up comin' in here. Caught a glimpse of Corrigan and O'Quinn goin' out the back door. Big O'Quinn was movin' pretty slow and Corrigan looked like he was draggin' Tim Durkan. Reckon I missed a hell of a fight between you and them fellers."

"Wish *I* had," the Gunsmith muttered.

"Oh, I found this gun lyin' over yonder." The hostler pulled a revolver from his belt.

"Only one?" Clint asked, taking the pistol.

" 'Fraid so, mate."

"Thank God they left mine." The Gunsmith managed a grin as he recognized the .45 Colt he had personally modified to fire double action. "Wherever they got to, those three are armed and desperate as hell."

"Reckon that makes them pretty much like the rest of us right now," Duffy mused. "You gonna help us fight the Limey and his bully-boys?"

"I'm gonna try to stop this mess before it gets that far," Clint replied, walking unsteadily to the door.

He opened it a crack and peered outside. The streets of Dublin seemed deserted, but he saw a group of armed men lurking behind an assortment of cover at the outskirts of town. Clint guessed John Hacker had organized the assault team. The gunmen had assumed good positions and no doubt were prepared to hit Dublin with a fourway crossfire.

"This is Major Huntington-Smythe," a familiar voice with a Cambridge accent declared. "I am ordering all of you to throw out your weapons and surrender immediately."

"Go to hell, you son of an English trollop!" an Irishman shouted in reply. "We not be givin' in to the likes of you!"

"You've got no right to do this!" another voice added.

"And what right have you to dynamite my mine and murder my men?" Huntington-Smythe demanded. "I've been patient with you people. I've tried to avoid bloodshed. Apparently that was a mistake."

"You're makin' your biggest mistake right now, Brit!" a defiant Irishman declared. "Pickin' a fight with the sons of the Emerald Island!"

"You barbarians only understand force," the Briton answered. "Very well. I'm through trying to reason with you—"

The Gunsmith opened the door and stepped from the

Glenmalure. He walked to the center of town to be certain everyone could see him clearly.

"Well, Mr. Adams." Huntington-Smythe chuckled. "I'm rather surprised to see you here. As a matter of fact, you and I still have something to discuss. I believe you have something that belongs to me. However, that is a personal matter and I'll deal with it later. For now, you'd best get out of the line of fire."

"He's right, Clint," the voice of Sean O'Hara called from his home. "It's too late for words to make a bit o' difference now."

"I'm certain we all admire your efforts to try to bring this business to a peaceful conclusion," the Englishman stated. "But it appears that was a waste of time for both of us."

"Don't talk about how you be wantin' peace, Brit," O'Hara shouted. "You call this invasion an act of peace?"

"It's self-defense," Huntington-Smythe replied. "You Irish attacked my mine today, so I have to make certain you never do it again."

"We didn't attack your goddamn mine!"

Slowly, not wishing to startle anyone into pulling a trigger by reflex reaction, the Gunsmith drew his Colt from leather. Clint extended his arm straight overhead and fired a single round into the sky.

"Do I have everybody's attention now?" he asked. "Good. Now everybody just shut up and listen to me."

"We've already heard enough from you, Mr. Adams," Huntington-Smythe replied.

"Aye," O'Hara added. "Talkin' ain't gonna help now!"

"So you two finally found something to agree about," Clint said dryly. "Well, if everybody is determined to kill each other, that's okay with me. But just let me say a couple things first. Hell, nobody's going any place for a while. Can't you wait a minute or two before you start shooting at each other?"

"Let's listen to Clint, Major," John Hacker's voice called out. "What can it hurt?"

"That's right," Duffy's reedy voice agreed. "Better hear what Clint's got to say."

Several others voiced support for the proposal. The Gunsmith waited until the shouts died down before he spoke.

"I've already told both Mayor O'Hara and Major Huntington-Smythe who is responsible for this feud," Clint began. "The Molly Maguires caused this. Maybe it would be more accurate to say three fellas who were Molly Maguires back in Pennsylvania are responsible.

"Corrigan, Durkan and O'Quinn are your real enemies," the Gunsmith continued. "And I'm talking to the people of Dublin as well as the major and his men. Those three sabotaged the mines, murdered the major's men and arranged for Malloy to get killed."

"That's a lie!" a woman's voice screamed, no doubt the wife of one of the trio.

"Take a look at me," Clint demanded. "I just had a fight with those three a few minutes ago. I confronted them with my evidence and tried to force them to confess."

The Gunsmith told the crowd about his encounter with Corrigan, O'Quinn and Durkan. He explained how he made his deductions about the Molly Maguires, and how Durkan had made his slip-of-the-lip about the masks. Clint then told them of Corrigan's confession about the scheme to seize control of both the mining company and the town.

"Lies!" the woman shrieked. "All lies!"

"If I'm lying why haven't Corrigan and the others stepped forward to state their side of the story?" Clint insisted.

"If you be tellin' the truth why haven't they shot you to shut you up?" an Irishman demanded.

"With all these witnesses about?" O'Hara snorted. "Don't be silly, Brian."

"Wait a minute," Clint declared. "I half expected them to take a shot at me when I first stepped into the center of town to talk to you people. After all, if I'd been shot all you Irish would have figured the major's men did it, and the major would have assumed one of the townsfolk killed me."

"Then why hasn't one of 'em tried to shoot you?" O'Hara asked.

"That's obvious," the Gunsmith answered. "They're no longer in Dublin."

"How'd they get past my men?" Huntington-Smythe asked.

"They're good at slipping in and out of town without attracting attention," Clint replied. "They've done it often enough. What matters is the fact they've started this feud and now they're counting on you folks killing each other so they can move in and take over.

"And all of you had better understand something," the Gunsmith continued. "Corrigan couldn't have succeeded as far as he already has unless he'd correctly predicted how you'd respond. You Irish refused to believe other Irishmen could be villains. Huntington-Smythe was too eager to blame this entire town because its residents are Irish. You've all reacted in exactly the narrow-minded manner that Corrigan wanted you to."

"Now, see here, Adams—" the Briton began.

"Corrigan used you people," Clint insisted. "He used your prejudice and hatred to get you to fight each other so he could claim his own selfish victory. Are you going to let him win, or join forces against your real enemy at last?"

A silence followed. It lasted only a few seconds, yet it seemed to be an eternity in that stress-charged atmosphere.

"Mr. O'Hara," Huntington-Smythe called out. "I would like to enter your town to speak with you and Mr. Adams. May I do so peaceably, sir?"

"Sure'n you may, Major," O'Hara confirmed as he emerged from his house, armed only with his walking stick. "Seems we should have agreed to meet and talk things out long ago, sir."

"Indeed," Huntington-Smythe agreed. He strolled into Dublin unarmed. "But right now we should decide what to do about this Corrigan chap."

"We'll have to find him first," O'Hara replied.

"I think I know where he's gone," the Gunsmith announced.

TWENTY-SIX

Doctor Riley, the local medical man in Dublin, treated Clint Adams' head wound. He fished out a couple of slivers of glass and applied iodine to the minor cuts in Clint's scalp. As the doctor bandaged his head, the Gunsmith told Sean O'Hara and Huntington-Smythe his theory about Corrigan and the other Molly Maguires.

"I figure they headed for the major's place," Clint explained.

"Why would they go there?" the Briton frowned.

"Because Corrigan and his partners were betting that there would be a big shooting match between your people and the citizens of Dublin," the Gunsmith declared. "They've obviously done some scouting 'round your spread. They know you've got more men who are better armed and more experienced with gunfights than the folks in Dublin. Corrigan didn't hang around here to help the townsfolk, so he obviously figured the major would win the fight."

"But didn't Corrigan try to convince you to join him to fight the Brit?" O'Hara asked. He glanced at Huntington-Smythe. "No offense, Major."

"None taken," the Englishman assured him.

"Corrigan was just trying to get me to drop my guard," the Gunsmith explained. "As soon as I put my gun away he would have jumped me. Corrigan's too clever to get into a face-to-face fight against superior odds. He probably figured a lot of the major's men would be killed in the battle here."

"Then we'd return home with our forces whittled down to a bit," Huntington-Smythe continued, "And we'd find an ambush waiting for us."

"Right," Clint nodded. "And we'd better assume they'll have something special planned. Probably a trap involving explosives."

"Durkan is an expert powderman," O'Hara added, for the Briton's sake.

"Then we'd best get after those three immediately," Huntington-Smythe declared.

"Aye," O'Hara agreed. "And more than one Irishman will be more than willin' to ride with you."

"That's a generous offer," the Briton replied. "But my property is under attack now. This isn't your fight, Mr. O'Hara."

"Some of our people are responsible," the Irishman stated.

"Can't blame you for that," the major shrugged.

"I see," O'Hara frowned. "Could it be you don't trust us to ride with you?"

"Oh, no." Clint sighed. "Don't start anything now, Sean. Not after we've managed to make peace."

"Nobody be lookin' for a fight, Clint," O'Hara assured him. "Except with Corrigan and his mates."

"Okay," the Gunsmith began. "We'd better split our forces into two groups—"

"Irish and English?" O'Hara asked.

"No," Clint groaned. "I was thinking of sending one group to the mines and the other to the major's spread. Corrigan's team will almost certainly be at one place or the other."

"Who'll be in charge?" Huntington-Smythe asked.

"How about you and I take command of the men who go to your ranch while Sean and Hacker check out the mines?"

"Sounds fair enough," the Briton agreed.

"I'd rather have you with me, Clint," O'Hara said. "I don't know this Hacker bloke."

"Well, I think it's more likely Corrigan will prepare his ambush at the major's home rather than the mines," the Gunsmith said. "I'd sort of like to be where I can do the most good."

"Then why don't we take our group to the major's spread and let him check the mines?" O'Hara pouted.

"Because it's my home," Huntington-Smythe answered.

"Well," O'Hara sighed, "all right. I'll take Hacker—whoever he is."

"He's a good man," Clint assured him. "He knows how to handle a firefight and he can handle men well. They'll listen to Hacker."

"You mean the men workin' for the major?" O'Hara asked. "Not the Irish from Dublin."

"Right," the Gunsmith confirmed. "They'll obey you. Together you should have a good team."

"Aye." O'Hara sighed. "But it not be likely we'll see any action, eh?"

"Maybe we'll get lucky and we'll be able to convince Corrigan to surrender without any more bloodshed," Clint remarked.

"A nice thought," Huntington-Smythe mused. "But do you honestly think it's very likely to happen?"

"No," the Gunsmith admitted.

TWENTY-SEVEN

The Gunsmith and Huntington-Smythe led a group of sixteen men, consisting of eleven employees of the Englishman and seven Irishmen. The Briton and Clint Adams rode side by side several yards in front of the others.

"I suppose you want to talk to me about Christine," the Gunsmith remarked.

"Now isn't the time to discuss it," Huntington-Smythe replied. "We'll talk later."

"After this is over Christine and I will be moving on together," Clint told him bluntly.

"You've got no right to take her," the Briton said sharply.

"And you've got no right to keep her, Major," Clint declared.

"The girl and I have an arrangement, Mister Adams," Huntington-Smythe stated.

Clint nodded. "She told me about that. I wouldn't say an indentured servant is the kind of contract that would hold up in court these days. Besides, Christine claims she has already completed her time, according to your agreement. Is that true?"

"I intend to discuss terms for a new contract with her."

"Does that mean marriage?"

"Don't be absurd," the Briton scoffed. "The girl is a servant. A gentleman of breeding doesn't marry someone of that class."

"You'll probably have trouble seeing where you're going if you don't stop doing that," the Gunsmith remarked.

"Doing what?" Huntington-Smythe frowned.

"Turning your nose up all the time," Clint explained. "That snotty, superior attitude of yours hasn't caused anything but trouble. Why don't you try to change it?"

"You can certainly be an offensive individual, Mr. Adams," the Englishman remarked. "Tell me, are you in love with Christine?"

"No," the Gunsmith answered. "But I don't want to own her either. Figure I'll take her to a large town where she can find a job, and eventually a husband."

"I suppose I can find someone to replace her." Huntington-Smythe shrugged. "And you deserve some sort of reward for all you've done. Very well, Mr. Adams. She's yours."

"Thanks," the Gunsmith muttered, staring at the surrounding rock walls. "How close are we to your spread?"

"Not far now," the Briton replied. "Less than half a mile. You'll be able to see the house when we get over that—"

The snarl of a rifle shot echoed from the rocks. A bullet hissed past Clint's face, actually tugging at the brim of his stetson. One of the men behind Clint screamed when the bullet slammed into his chest, and then he tumbled, lifeless, from his saddle.

"Scatter!" Clint shouted. "Run for cover!"

The Gunsmith swatted Duke's rump, a signal that

DYNAMITE JUSTICE

the gelding was supposed to seek shelter. Duke's uncanny instincts and incredible speed took over. The horse galloped to a large cone-shaped boulder, big enough to provide cover for Duke and the Gunsmith.

"Nice work, big fella," Clint said, patting the gelding's neck.

Duke neighed softly and nodded his head in reply.

The Gunsmith swung down from the saddle and drew his Springfield carbine from its boot. He heard several shots explode as he moved to the edge of the boulder. Clint cautiously peered around the corner.

Five men on horseback were still trying to find adequate cover. Three other men no longer needed to worry. They lay dead with bullet holes in their chests.

Clint spotted the muzzle flash of two rifles along the rock walls. The Molly Maguires had clearly selected their cover in advance. Corrigan planned well. The Gunsmith couldn't even locate the barrel of a sniper's rifle.

An explosion erupted about a hundred yards from Clint's position. He saw chunks of rock hurled from the mountain wall across from the killer's position. Men screamed as stones crashed down on them.

"Jesus," Clint rasped. "The bastards suckered us into a trap!"

Another explosion sent a second shower of rocks tumbling down on the Gunsmith's posse. More men screamed. Others bolted in fear and exposed themselves to sniper fire. The enemy rifles roared and bullets smashed into two more victims.

Clint aimed his Springfield at the muzzle flash of a sniper's weapon. He triggered the carbine. A forty-five slug sparked as it struck stone, or possibly the barrel of the assassin's rifle.

Suddenly the bulky figure of Mike O'Quinn rose up

from behind a boulder. The big man held a rifle in one hand as he pawed at his face with the other. He'd probably been struck by a piece of flying rock, the same way Clint had received the scar on his left cheek years ago.

The Gunsmith quickly worked the lever of his carbine. A spent shell casing popped from the breech and a fresh round snapped into the chamber. He aimed and fired.

A bullet shattered Mike O'Quinn's face. His skull exploded in a grisly burst of blood and brains which splattered the rock wall. O'Quinn's corpse slumped behind the boulder and vanished from view.

Another rifle cracked. A bullet whined against the Gunsmith's stone shelter. Clint ducked behind his cover and glanced around the edge of the boulder. He saw a figure scramble up the rock wall. The man's left arm dangled loosely. Blood stained his shirt sleeve.

Someone fired a shot at the retreating sniper. The bullet chipped stone more than a foot from the fleeing Molly Maguire. Clint saw the man's face as he crawled over the summit of the mountain. It was Jack Corrigan.

The shooting ceased. Through the ringing of his ears he could hear the groans of wounded men and the drumlike throb of the pulse behind his ear.

"Clint!" a voice called hoarsely. "Clint, can you hear me? They didn't kill you, did they?"

The Gunsmith didn't reply because he couldn't hear the voice well enough to recognize it. For all he knew, everyone else in his group had been killed and Timothy Durkan was trying to lure him out of his shelter. What about the shot fired at Corrigan? Could be a clever trick to make Clint think the Molly Maguires had been driven off by survivors of his group.

"Clint, this is Stan Struthers," the voice declared. "I'm coming toward you so don't shoot me."

"Watch yourself, Stan," the Gunsmith warned. "The bastards might be waiting for us to get careless."

Silently, Clint warned himself to heed his own advice.

The stocky figure of Stan Struthers soon appeared at Clint's position. His ten gallon hat was gone and blood trickled from a gash above his left temple. Stan managed a weak smile.

"You purely got a charmed life, Clint," the cowboy remarked. "How'd you manage to get to such a good place for cover?"

"A little help from my friend," the Gunsmith replied, patting Duke. "How bad were we hit?"

"Not good," Stan frowned. "Most of our men were killed. Everybody else is wounded, except you."

"What about Huntington-Smythe?" Clint asked.

"A rock broke his leg," Stan answered. "Major ain't gonna be able to ride. Neither will most of the others. Hell, there's only about five or six horses left anyway . . . and we'll have to find most of those critters. The animals took off like bats outta hell when that dynamite went off."

"Christ, what a mess." The Gunsmith shook his head. "And we rode right into it."

"Can't blame yourself for that, Clint."

"I don't," the Gunsmith assured him. "I blame Jack Corrigan. Well, the Molly Maguires didn't escape without some casualties, either. O'Quinn is dead and Corrigan was wounded. Didn't see Durkan, so we'd better assume he's alive and still in one piece."

"Figure they'll head on to the major's place?" Stan asked.

"Yeah," Clint replied. "But you'd better stay here and protect the wounded just in case I'm wrong. The bastards might come back to finish what they started."

"You don't plan to go after them jaspers by yourself, do you?" Stan asked, staring at the Gunsmith as if he thought Clint had lost his mind.

"Like you said," Clint answered. "I'm the only man who wasn't injured. I can move faster without having to slow my pace for the sake of a wounded partner. Won't have to worry about anybody but myself when I catch up with Corrigan."

"There's gotta be another way," Stan insisted.

The Gunsmith shrugged. "Maybe there is. But there isn't time to consider it. I'm going after Corrigan and I'm going right now."

TWENTY-EIGHT

Clint Adams saw the major's house in the distance. He tugged Duke's reins and urged the horse to a halt. The Gunsmith reached for his Dolland and patted Duke's neck.

"So far, so-so," he told the gelding.

Duke snorted a neutral reply.

The Gunsmith had left Stan Struthers and the other survivors of the ambush to continue to stalk the killers alone. The horrible vision of the bullet-riddled and crushed corpses of men who had been part of the posse haunted Clint as he rode along the pass toward Huntington-Smythe's property. The grisly images did not interrupt Clint's concentration. They served as a grim reminder that he must remain alert, and added fuel to his determination to hunt down Corrigan and Durkan.

The Molly Maguires had not launched another attack. This strengthened Clint's suspicion that the murderous pair must have headed for the ranch. The Gunsmith figured they'd probably hole up inside the house. He slid open the pocket telescope and started to raise it to his eye.

Then the house exploded.

Huntington-Smythe's home was torn apart by the

blast. The brown stone walls burst into a meteor shower. The tile roof hurled into the sky. Debris scattered across the ground and flames crackled amid what was left.

"My god," the Gunsmith exclaimed as he examined the site through his Dolland.

One minute a house existed. The next it was gone and only a charred pile of rubble remained. Clint scanned the surrounding terrain for any sign of the Molly Maguires. Something was moving in the distance.

Clint shifted his telescope and trained it on two men on horseback. Although their backs were turned to Clint, he was certain they were Corrigan and Durkan. They rode their mounts hard, heading for the hills beyond.

"The mines," Clint rasped. "Those bastards plan to destroy everything. . . ."

He urged Duke into a full gallop and gave chase. The pair had almost a mile headstart. Even Duke couldn't run fast enough to catch up with the enemy horsemen unless their animals tired.

What worried Clint wasn't that the pair would escape or that they'd turn and fight. The Gunsmith did not fear any man in a face-to-face gunfight. He'd be more than willing to take on both Corrigan and Durkan at the same time under such conditions.

But Clint realized the Mollies wouldn't fight him on his terms. If Corrigan and Durkan realized the Gunsmith was in pursuit, they'd probably try to set up another ambush. Fighting pistols was Clint's specialty. Not fighting dynamite.

The two killers galloped toward the base of a hill. Clint saw their objective. Corrigan and Durkan were heading for one of the mines.

DYNAMITE JUSTICE

The Mollies' horses had slowed their pace, but Duke continued to run. Clint urged the gelding to decrease his speed slightly when he saw a congregation of armed horsemen approach the mine from the west. The posse led by Sean O'Hara and John Hacker had arrived.

The two Molly Maguires and the posse immediately exchanged shots. Durkan's horse shrieked and collapsed, throwing its rider to the ground. Two members of the posse were also hit and fell from their saddles, clutching at the bullet wounds in their chests.

Corrigan dismounted. He drew his pistol and fired as he ran to his fallen comrade. Durkan did not appear to be injured by his fall. The little Irishman rolled to the cover of a large metal ore car set on the rails extending from the mouth of the mine. Clint saw Durkan reach into a canvas knapsack slung over his shoulder.

Dynamite, the Gunsmith realized.

Durkan struck a match against the iron frame of the ore car and held the flame to the abbreviated fuse on a stick of dynamite. He hurled the explosive in a high overhand throw, lobbing it at the posse.

Men and horses scattered in all directions. One rider actually galloped toward the dynamite. It exploded under the horse, tearing man and animal to pieces. Other horses rose up on their hind legs and tossed more riders. One fell, rolling over its owner, breaking bones beneath its crushing weight.

Clint brought Duke to a halt as he watched Corrigan dash to the cover of the ore car. Both men crouched behind their shelter. Durkan opened his knapsack to extract more dynamite. The posse bolted for the cover of nearby boulders, concerned only with their own survival.

The Gunsmith drew his Springfield carbine from its boot. He put the buttstock to his shoulder and aimed carefully. The front sight of the carbine divided Durkan's head as the Irishman lit the fuse to another stick of dynamite.

Durkan suddenly shifted to the right as he prepared to hurl the explosive. Clint swung the Springfield to follow the target's movement and squeezed the trigger. A forty-five slug smashed into Durkan's left shoulder blade. The Irishman's body twisted violently from the impact of the bullet as he awkwardly tossed the dynamite.

It left his fingers and sailed into the open top of the ore car. Jack Corrigan hastily leaped up and reached into the car to retrieve the explosive stick. Clint desperately worked the lever action of his carbine. Corrigan straightened his back and raised the stick of dynamite in his right fist.

Then it exploded. The blast detonated several more sticks in Durkan's knapsack. The tremendous explosion hurled the ore car twenty feet into the sky. Dust and debris spewed in all directions like the petals of an enormous, macabre flower.

When the grimy cloud settled, all that remained of Jack Corrigan and Timothy Durkan was a crater in the earth. There wasn't enough left of their bodies to fill a shoebox.

TWENTY-NINE

"How's the leg, Major?" the Gunsmith asked Huntington-Smythe after Doc Riley finished setting a splint on the broken limb.

"A bloody wreck," he replied through clenched teeth. "Like everything else. Those bastards killed more than a dozen of my men today. They destroyed my house and blew up a mineshaft."

"Yeah," Clint agreed, "but you won't have to worry about the three guys responsible for it anymore. You can rebuild and open the mine again. The coal is making a profit, right?"

"True," Huntington-Smythe admitted. "But I'll need more men to mine for it now."

"I think you know where to find them," the Gunsmith remarked. "Don't you?"

"Yes, indeed," the Englishman replied.

Sean O'Hara entered the doctor's home. He had just finished telling several women that their husbands had been killed. The mayor's expression was somber, but he politely inquired about Huntington-Smythe's condition.

"Broken leg," the Briton told him. "It'll mend in time. Like to talk to you about a couple things, Mr. O'Hara."

"If you're concerned about havin' a roof over your

head, you've nothin' to fear, Major," O'Hara assured him. "You're welcome to stay here until we rebuild your house."

"My house?" the Briton's monocle slipped when he raised his eyebrow.

The Irishman nodded. "Aye. Jack Corrigan was our best carpenter but we've several other lads who are handy with wood, stone and mortar. We've not been very good neighbors to each other in the past, Major, but we want to change that. Seems that rebuildin' your house would be a good place to start."

"I say," Huntington-Smythe began, "that's quite good of you. I'll pay your chaps for their labor and construction material, of course."

"No need for that," O'Hara said. "We can't leave you homeless. Besides, I imagine most of your money was destroyed when your house blew up."

"Nonsense," the major replied. "I keep most of it in a bank in Denver."

"Still, I think it proper that we rebuild the house without pay," O'Hara insisted. "Not right that a man be without a home."

"But I insist," the Briton told him.

"Why don't you fellas compromise?" Clint suggested. "The major can pay for the materials and make a contribution to the widows in Dublin."

"That's a bloody good idea, Mr. Adams," Huntington-Smythe declared. "And I'd also like to offer employment to any of your people who want to work for my mining company. The miners already in my service will tell you I pay well, and the conditions in the mine are as good as possible. Your people will receive the same salary and the same sort of treatment. You have my word on that."

DYNAMITE JUSTICE 175

"By God you've got yourself a deal, Major." O'Hara smiled. "Looks like there'll be some good come of this after all."

"And we owe a great deal of thanks to Mr. Adams for that," the Briton stated.

"Aye, Clint," the Irishman said. "Sure'n you should get somethin' in return for all you've done for us."

"Everything is fine with me," the Gunsmith assured him.

"Mr. Adams is taking a prize with him." The major smiled, taking his wallet from a pocket. "I've got a hundred dollars here. Give it to Christine to help her make a new start."

"I will," Clint told him as Huntington-Smythe handed the Gunsmith several twenty dollar bills.

"Christine, eh?" O'Hara grinned. "Seems you have got a way with the ladies, Clint. Kate Malloy was askin' 'bout you. Real concerned she seemed, too."

"I'm not much for farewells," the Gunsmith said. "Will you tell her good-bye for me?"

"Sure," O'Hara agreed. "Want I should tell the same to Bridgett O'Quinn?"

"That treacherous bitch?" Clint rolled his eyes at the ceiling. "You've gotta be kidding, Sean."

"Bridgett asked me to tell you she was sorry about how she tried to set you up for her husband," O'Hara declared. "Said she wouldn't have done it if Mike hadn't threatened her if she failed to oblige."

"Say whatever you want to Bridgett," the Gunsmith answered. "I'm getting out of here and this time I'm not coming back."

"Not ever, Mr. Adams?" Huntington-Smythe inquired. "I certainly hope that isn't the case."

"Maybe I'll swing by here some time in the future," Clint replied. "Might be interesting to see what kind of place you folks will make now that you're trying to get along with each other."

"Nobody would be sorry if'n you stayed, Clint," O'Hara told him.

"At least one person would regret it," Clint said.

"And who would that be?" the Irishman asked.

"Me," the Gunsmith replied.

THIRTY

The Gunsmith and Christine arrived at the town of Fillmore that evening shortly after sunset. Clint took the wagon and horses to the local livery stable.

"Now that you've taken care of your rig and those horses," Christine began, inserting her arm into the crook of Clint's elbow, "can we go to the hotel?"

"I usually let the local lawman know I'm in town first," the Gunsmith replied. "But that can wait until morning."

"Is something bothering you, Clint?" she asked.

"It's probably nothing."

"So why not tell me what it is?"

" 'Cause I'll sound like a silly, nervous ninny," the Gunsmith answered.

"If you don't tell me about it I'll worry too," she said.

"Well"—Clint sighed—"I was just thinking that Mike O'Quinn seemed to be pretty good with a rifle when the Molly Maguires ambushed the posse."

"So?" the confused girl asked.

"So why did he use a shotgun instead of a rifle when he tried to ambush me the other day?" Clint explained. "A rifle would have been a more logical choice. The shotgun didn't have a long enough range to do the job."

"Maybe O'Quinn used a shotgun to try to make it look as if somebody else had tried to kill you," Christine suggested.

"Since the major's men had already shot at me with rifles in that same ravine," Clint began, "I'd figure a shotgun would seem more suspicious."

Christine shrugged. "I guess O'Quinn was just plain stupid."

"You're probably right," the Gunsmith agreed. "Let's get that hotel room and try to forget about everything but each other for a while."

"Now you're making sense, Clint," she said with a laugh.

The couple strolled along the plankwalk to the hotel, unaware that a pair of hard black eyes followed their progress.

When they entered the building a tall, husky figure emerged from an alley and limped across the street, his right foot stomping the ground with every step.

"How long will we be staying here?" Christine asked Clint as she sprawled across the brass-framed bed.

"In Fillmore?" the Gunsmith inquired, unbuckling his gunbelt.

"In this hotel room," the girl replied with a sly smile.

"That'll depend on how business turns out. Probably only a day or two."

She frowned. "Then you'll be moving on?"

"We've already discussed this, Christine," he told

her as he hung the gunbelt over the headboard of the bed.

"I know." She sighed. "We can enjoy our time together, but we have to realize it's only gonna last for a little while."

"Christine," the Gunsmith began, "it's better to have some warm, beautiful memories to recall from a brief, pleasant encounter than to have a long-term involvement that ends in bitterness and disappointment."

"Are you so sure that always happens?" Christine asked.

"I'm sure there's no future for you with me," Clint told her.

"Really, Clint," she rolled her eyes. "Do you honestly think somebody will always be trying to kill you because you're the Gunsmith? Don't you think that's sort of an exaggeration?"

"Honey—" he began, but a knock on the door interrupted him.

Clint quickly plucked his .45 Colt from its holster. Christine sighed and shook her head, dismayed by his overreaction. The Gunsmith moved to the door.

"Who is it?" he asked.

"The desk clerk, sir," a voice replied nervously.

"What do you want?" Clint inquired. "Didn't I bribe you enough to let me bring a girl up to my room?"

"It's not that, sir," the clerk said awkwardly. "There'—there's a problem I want to ask you about."

"Oh, hell," the Gunsmith muttered as he reached for the doorknob.

Without warning, the door seemed to explode. It

crashed into Clint with staggering force. The Gunsmith was hurled across the room by the impact. Christine screamed. Clint fell against a wall, the Colt revolver knocked out of his grasp.

A huge man limped into the room; he smiled coldly as he aimed his sawed-off shotgun at the Gunsmith. The desk clerk's body lay sprawled across the threshold between the giant's splayed legs.

"Bonsoir, Monsieur Adams. We meet again, *oui?"*

"Jules," Clint replied, stunned as he recognized his assailant. "I thought I'd seen the last of you back in New Orleans."*

"I escaped from the hospital before they could send me to prison," the giant told him. *"Monsieur* Lacombe and most of the others were hanged, but the police did not get me. I waited until my bones healed—and then I began to stalk you."

"Clint . . ." Christine began in a horrified voice.

"Don't panic," the Gunsmith replied. "Jules doesn't have any reason to want to hurt you. I'm the one he wants."

"Oui." The Frenchman smiled. "I've hunted you for more than a year. Throughout the West I heard stories about *l'Armurier*. Each time I learned where you had been, it gave me a clue as to where you might be going."

"And you almost got me the other day in the ravine."

Jules nodded. "That's right. If those other men hadn't come to your rescue, I would have killed you then. Just as well. I want to see your face when you die, Adams. I want you to know who killed you and why."

---

* *The Gunsmith #23: The Riverboat Gang*

DYNAMITE JUSTICE

The Gunsmith shrugged. "Okay. Go ahead and pull the trigger. I'm just disappointed that you don't have enough guts to fight me like a man."

"You think I'd let you have a gun?" Jules snorted. "That would be absurd, *oui?*"

"I figured you'd be willing to fight with just hands and feet," Clint explained. "After all, you're a lot bigger than me, and you're supposed to be such a great expert at French kick-boxing. But I guess folks were just afraid of that steel foot you've got. They don't know how slow and clumsy you really are."

"*Cochon!*" Jules hissed. "I could crush you like an insect!"

"Didn't work out that way the last time. I kicked the shit out of you. Remember?"

"You were lucky," Jules stated. "If you hadn't thrown sand in my eyes . . ."

"There's no sand in this room," the Gunsmith told him. "How about a rematch, Jules? What's the matter? Scared I'll take you again?"

Jules smiled. "It would be a pleasure to stomp the life from your body. Ah, but wait! I know your tricks. Remove your shirt first."

"I'm not carrying the New Line Colt," the Gunsmith said, referring to a small hideout pistol he often wore under his shirt.

"Do as I tell you," the giant snarled. "And do so slowly or I'll splatter you all over the wall with a load of buckshot."

Clint unbuttoned his shirt and slipped it off. Jules broke open his shotgun and dumped the shells onto the floor.

"Very well, Adams." The Frenchman smiled. "Shall we begin?"

Jules suddenly hurled the empty shotgun at Clint, striking him in the chest. Clint groaned, fell into the wall and slid to the floor. Jules closed in fast and lashed his steel foot at the Gunsmith's face.

Clint weaved his head aside. Jules kicked the wall. Plaster burst from the impact and cracks jutted around the damaged section. The Gunsmith didn't try to grab Jules's ankle, aware the giant was too strong to be thrown off balance. Instead he rolled away from his opponent and scrambled to his feet.

Jules attacked again, his deadly right foot swinging a high roundhouse kick at Clint's head. The Gunsmith jumped back to avoid the kick, which would have shattered his skull if it connected.

The steel foot hit the floor; Jules pivoted on it and suddenly thrust out his left leg in a fast sidekick. The foot slammed into Clint's chest and propelled him six feet into another wall.

Christine bravely attacked Jules. She held the empty shotgun by its twin barrels and swung the stock like a club. The giant caught the shotgun and easily yanked it from the girl's grasp. He swatted the back of a hand across Christine's face, knocking her to the floor. Jules tossed the shotgun aside and turned to face Clint.

This time Jules wasn't fast enough. Clint swung a boot at Jules's groin. The kick struck the giant in the gut and Jules bent slightly and grunted in pain. Clint clasped both hands together and smashed them into his opponent's face.

Jules's head twisted from the blow, but he swung a backfist at Clint. The Gunsmith caught the Frenchman's arm and shoved the heel of his left palm into Jules's elbow to lock the arm as he quickly lashed another kick to the giant's abdomen. Jules groaned in pain. Clint kicked him again. The brute doubled up with a grunt.

The Gunsmith released his opponent's arm and again clasped his hands together. He chopped his doubled fists into the nape of Jules's neck. When the Frenchman fell to all fours, Clint kicked him in the ribs.

Suddenly, Jules lashed out his right leg like an alligator's tail. The low sweep struck Clint's ankles and kicked his feet from the floor. He fell, then rolled and sprang to his feet as Jules once again rose from the floor.

Clint was astonished by the amount of punishment his huge adversary could absorb. Blood oozed from Jules's mouth as he grinned and threw a steel-footed kick at Clint's groin. The Gunsmith dodged the attack and hit Jules in the jaw with a solid left hook.

He swung a right cross. Clint's punch was blocked by Jules's left forearm. The giant's right fist crashed into the Gunsmith's face and sent him toppling onto the bed. He lay on the mattress as the room whirled before his dazed eyes.

Jules shouted in victory and leaped feet-first at the bed, aiming his double-stomp at the Gunsmith. Clint quickly rolled off the mattress. Under the impact of Jules's stomp, the bedsprings shattered, the mattress collapsed and the bedframe sagged feebly.

Clint snatched his gunbelt from the headboard, wishing the holster wasn't empty. Jules leaped from the broken bed to confront the Gunsmith. Clint swung the belt in a vicious backhand stroke. The French killer screamed when the buckle slashed his right cheek to the bone.

The Gunsmith swung the belt again. Jules ducked

under the whirling buckle only to receive a boot in the face. Clint's kick staggered the giant and set him up for a diagonal belt stroke. The buckle ripped a gash in Jules's left brow and sliced his eyeball. Blood poured from the eyesocket and Jules roared in agony and fury.

The Frenchman launched a furious sidekick at his opponent. Clint sidestepped and the steel foot struck a windowpane. Glass exploded. Jules staggered forward awkwardly, thrown off balance by the momentum of his own kick when it failed to connect with a solid object.

The Gunsmith moved behind his opponent and simply shoved Jules. The giant fell against the wall, his right leg thrust through the window. His buttock hit the windowsill and Clint quickly wrapped his gunbelt around Jules's neck.

The Frenchman struggled violently as the Gunsmith applied pressure to the improvised garrote. Jules tried to jab his elbows into Clint's ribs. Clint raised his knee sharply and rammed it between the big man's splayed legs. Jules shrieked and twisted his body to try to pull his trapped leg free.

Clint held on and continued to throttle the French brute. Jules kicked out with his left foot, trying to shove himself and his adversary backward, away from the window.

His left foot shattered more glass. Clint pushed hard. Both Jules's legs disappeared out the window. The Gunsmith was suddenly yanked forward as the giant's body plunged outside. Clint hit the window frame and braced his feet against the wall. His arms were almost yanked out of their sockets by the weight of the Frenchman whom he still held onto by the belt wrapped around Jules's neck.

DYNAMITE JUSTICE

Bone snapped.

Clint wondered if it might be one of his. Then he gazed down at the slowly swaying body of his opponent. Jules's head hung loosely to one side. The giant's neck had been broken as if in a hangman's noose. Clint released one end of the belt and allowed Jules's corpse to fall to the ground below.

"Clint!" Christine cried as she moved to his side. "Are you all right?"

"I'm alive," he said breathlessly, sitting on the floor in utter exhaustion. "Right now that's good enough."

A number of hotel guests appeared at the doorway. The desk clerk groaned as he recovered consciousness. A man with a badge pinned to his vest pushed his way through the crowd. The lawman stared at the wrecked room in amazement.

"Sweet Jesus," he gasped. "What in hell happened?"

"Fella outside," the Gunsmith replied, still panting hard. "He sort of hung around this hotel too long."

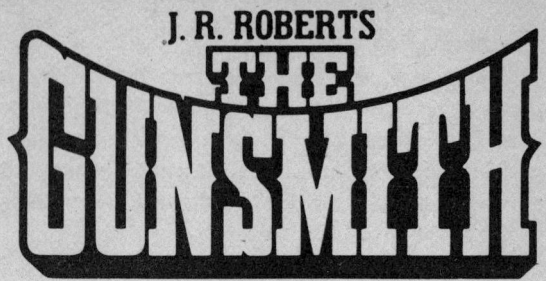

J. R. ROBERTS
THE GUNSMITH
SERIES

☐ 30928-3 THE GUNSMITH #1: MACKLIN'S WOMEN		$2.50
☐ 30878-3 THE GUNSMITH #2: THE CHINESE GUNMEN		$2.50
☐ 30858-9 THE GUNSMITH #3: THE WOMAN HUNT		$2.25
☐ 30925-9 THE GUNSMITH #5: THREE GUNS FOR GLORY		$2.50
☐ 30861-9 THE GUNSMITH #6: LEADTOWN		$2.25
☐ 30862-7 THE GUNSMITH #7: THE LONGHORN WAR		$2.25
☐ 30901-1 THE GUNSMITH #8: QUANAH'S REVENGE		$2.50
☐ 30923-2 THE GUNSMITH #9: HEAVYWEIGHT GUN		$2.50
☐ 30924-0 THE GUNSMITH #10: NEW ORLEANS FIRE		$2.50
☐ 30931-3 THE GUNSMITH #11: ONE-HANDED GUN		$2.50
☐ 30926-7 THE GUNSMITH #12: THE CANADIAN PAYROLL		$2.50
☐ 30927-5 THE GUNSMITH #13: DRAW TO AN INSIDE DEATH		$2.50
☐ 30922-4 THE GUNSMITH #14: DEAD MAN'S HAND		$2.50
☐ 30905-4 THE GUNSMITH #15: BANDIT GOLD		$2.50

Prices may be slightly higher in Canada.

Available at your local bookstore or return this form to:

CHARTER BOOKS
Book Mailing Service
P.O. Box 690, Rockville Centre, NY 11571

Please send me the titles checked above. I enclose _____. Include 75¢ for postage and handling if one book is ordered; 25¢ per book for two or more not to exceed $1.75. California, Illinois, New York and Tennessee residents please add sales tax.

NAME _____

ADDRESS _____

CITY _____ STATE/ZIP _____

(allow six weeks for delivery.)

A1